Samuel French Acting Edition

I Take This Man

by Jack Sharkey

SAMUELFRENCH.COM   SAMUELFRENCH.CO.UK

ISBN 978-0-573-69246-8

www.SamuelFrench.com
www.SamuelFrench.co.uk

FOR PRODUCTION ENQUIRIES

UNITED STATES AND CANADA
Info@SamuelFrench.com
1-866-598-8449

UNITED KINGDOM AND EUROPE
Plays@SamuelFrench.co.uk
020-7255-4302

Each title is subject to availability from Samuel French, depending upon country of performance. Please be aware that *I TAKE THIS MAN* may not be licensed by Samuel French in your territory. Professional and amateur producers should contact the nearest Samuel French office or licensing partner to verify availability.

MUSIC USE NOTE

Licensees are solely responsible for obtaining formal written permission from copyright owners to use copyrighted music in the performance of this play and are strongly cautioned to do so. If no such permission is obtained by the licensee, then the licensee must use only original music that the licensee owns and controls. Licensees are solely responsible and liable for all music clearances and shall indemnify the copyright owners of the play(s) and their licensing agent, Samuel French, against any costs, expenses, losses and liabilities arising from the use of music by licensees. Please contact the appropriate music licensing authority in your territory for the rights to any incidental music.

IMPORTANT BILLING AND CREDIT REQUIREMENTS

If you have obtained performance rights to this title, please refer to your licensing agreement for important billing and credit requirements.

CHARACTERS

GIDEON, a lovely young Bostonian lady
BRET, a handsome young Bostonian man
CHARLENE, a young and beautiful nurse
DEX, Charlene's good-looking fiance
JUD, a pleasantly helpful policeman

TIME

The third Monday in April, just this year

PLACE

The Back Bay section of Boston; specifically, a charming apartment in a converted townhouse.

ACT I: very late in the afternoon
ACT II: just under two seconds later

[NOTE: For certain comedic reasons (which will become crystally clear the moment you read the final two words in Charlene's second speech), your cast-listing in your programs should identify the characters *only* by their "given names" as above, with the names of their portrayers.]

I Take This Man had its world premiere on September 15, 1991, at the Ramada London Bridge Resort in Lake Havasu City, Arizona, via the Drury Lane Repertory Players, with the following cast:

GIDEON........................Tara Ann Bucchino
JUD ....Don Gunnarsson
BRET ....John Tracy
CHARLENE..........................Jodee Barnes
DEXTER ....Tom "Fritz" Erikson

Assistant Director: Tammy Aquin
Stage Manager: Donna Lou Lemaster
Lighting Technicians: Nikki Shacham, Jere Hoyt

ACT I

*The living room of GIDEON HOLLIS's apartment [see
Stage Setting], late afternoon. Decor is tasteful and
attractive but not expensive. Room is late-springtime-
afternoon sunny. This will shortly change.*

*AT RISE: Stage is empty. After a moment we hear key in
lock of front door, and then GIDDY opens door,
struggles her key out of lock, and calls back [L] down
hallway as she does so:*

GIDDY. That's it Officer! Right this way. I'll get
things ready! (*Rushes to armchair, takes throw-pillow off it
and another two from L end of sofa, mounds them on
cushion at R end of sofa; turns, sees open magazine on
armchair, picks it up, looks about for place to put it,
shrugs, then lifts armchair-cushion, tosses magazine
underneath it, and is just replacing cushion and
straightening up as JUD and BRET arrive at open doorway
to apartment.*) Oh you made it! Here, bring him right over
here, Officer! (*She says that because JUD is carrying BRET
over his shoulder; JUD is a uniformed policeman of middle
age; BRET is a younger man, blissfully unconscious,
wearing only a tank-top, shorts, shoes and socks and
nothing else*)
JUD. (*Moving toward her*) Over where?
GIDDY. On the sofa. The fabric's *Scotch-Garded*, and
he's all sweaty.
JUD. Don't you want him in the *bedroom*?

7

GIDDY. No. I just washed the sheets. He'll be better here. Besides, you've gone to *enough* trouble just toting him up all those *stairs*!

JUD. (*Will lay BRET on sofa, his head on pillows, R, during:*) Are you *sure*, miss? The poor guy needs a rest!

GIDDY. Honestly, the sofa's just fine! There! He looks *perfectly* comfortable! And I'll get him a blanket or something so he doesn't catch cold.

JUD. I don't feel right about this—I *ought* to take him to a *hospital*!

GIDDY. Aw, but you *know* what'll happen *there*, Officer! They'll check him over, then tell me he should be *home* getting some *rest*, and charge me a hundred-thirty-five dollars for the information! And then he'll be mad at me for spending the money. And—

JUD. Even so—when a citizen collapses in the street, I'm *supposed* to take him to the nearest medical facility—!

GIDDY. (*Moves close to him. Turning It On*) But people *always* collapse at the *Boston Marathon*, Officer, and aren't the hospitals always complaining about *overcrowding* with unnecessary patients, and—!

JUD. Okay-okay, you've made your point. But if my *partner* finds out I left the *car*—

GIDDY. Who's going to *tell* him? *I* certainly won't!

JUD. (*Scanning BRET*) You *sure* he's gonna be all right? He looks so *pale* ...

GIDDY. It's nice of you to be so concerned, but if *I'm* not worried, why should *you* be? My husband will be just fine, Officer, with a little rest. Now, shouldn't you be getting back to your patrol car? Your partner will be starting to wonder.

JUD. Well, you're right about *that*—hope Sam didn't *see* me trotting off with your husband. One of us should be near the car at all times in case a call comes in—but since your place is only two blocks from Copley Square, I figured I could get back in about ten minutes.

GIDDY. (*Trying to usher him to the door*) And you can if you hurry! So, thank you very much for your help, and—

JUD. Wait, not so fast, I've got to have your name for my report.

GIDDY. What report? I thought you weren't *going* to report this?

JUD. Well, I'm not if I don't *have* to—but if anybody saw me, and some questions get asked, I'd better have the facts all ready, just in case.

GIDDY. Oh ... all right. What do you have to know?

JUD. (*Takes out notebook and pencil*) Your name—?

GIDDY. Gideon Hollis.

JUD. That's a *man's* name, isn't it?

GIDDY. Daddy wanted a boy, so he did the next best thing. My friends call me "Giddy."

JUD. (*Will notate pertinent facts during dialogue, but not persiflage*) Okay, got it. Occupation?

GIDDY. Assistant Curator at the Museum of Fine Arts.

JUD. You or your husband?

GIDDY. Me. It's very handy. Only about a fifteen-minute *walk* from here, so I don't have to worry about parking a car or—

JUD. (*This reminds him*) *Car*! I've really got to get back and help Sam with crowd-control till the mob disperses. Just one more thing—what does your husband do?

GIDDY. (*Slightly uncomfortable, hesitates; then:*) He's a househusband. Does the shopping, cleaning, like that, and I make the living for both of us. I—I suppose you think that's highly unusual.

JUD. (*Closing notebook, putting it and pencil away*) Mmmm, no. Not nowadays, anyhow. But I *do* find it *baffling*. Why a strong, strapping male like your husband would stay home, while *you*— Oh, unless he's got something chronic, maybe, like a bad back or something? Like I said before, he *does* look extremely *white* around the face and neck. Are you *sure* you wouldn't want to have the hospital check him over, just in case—?

GIDDY. He *always* gets pale after physical exertion. Low blood-pressure. Believe me, if I thought there was the *slightest* chance he was anything more than simply pooped from running, I would have *insisted* you take him to the hospital!

JUD. (*Half-sold, backing doorward*) Well ... I guess ... okay! But—just to ease my mind—I think I'll drop by later on after I get off duty to see how he's doing, ma'am.

GIDDY. (*Hiding a tinge of dismay*) But you don't have to—

JUD. Oh, yes I do. I'm a worrier.

GIDDY. Well ... how *much* later on—?

JUD. Well, let's see—I get off duty at eight, so—oh—maybe about nine o'clock?

GIDDY. *Tonight?!*

JUD. Why *not* tonight?

GIDDY. It's—it's our wedding anniversary. One year ago today, exactly. We might be—out on the town!

JUD. In the shape *he's* in?

GIDDY. My husband is a quick recoverer. A little nap and he'll be raring to go!

JUD. (*At door now, hand on knob, still facing her*) I'm sorry, ma'am. Rules are rules. I *have* to check on him! I'd feel personally *responsible* if he had a relapse or anything!

GIDDY. But if we're not *here* ...?

JUD. (*Shrugs*) Then I'll know he must be okay, and it'll be a load off my mind!

GIDDY. That's—very conscientious of you, Officer ... um ...?

JUD. Keegan. Jud Keegan. If you need help—I'm as near as your telephone! Take it easy, ma'am. And have a good time tonight—(*Peeks past her toward BRET., shakes his head*)—but I doubt it very much. (*Shuts door and is gone*)

GIDDY. (*Leans back against door, blows out her cheeks in an audible sigh of relief, then shakes her head, straightens up, moves to sofa, and looks down at BRET a second, finally deciding aloud:*) You ought to be under a blanket! (*Exits to bedroom; we hear her humming happily offstage, and then she returns with a fluffy comforter which she places over him up to his chin, and turns to see that he's uncovered from the knees down*) You're so *darn* long-legged! I'm surprised you didn't come in *first* in that race! (*She takes off to the bedroom, humming happily again; a moment later, we hear a key in the lock and CHARLENE LOCKWOOD enters, removing key from lock, doffing light topcoat and hanging it on coat rack, replacing keys in her purse and hanging purse by its strap over topcoat; as she turns, GIDDY re-enters with larger coverlet, which she instantly tries to hide behind her back as she reacts to CHARLENE's presence with a little gasp*)

CHARLENE. *My*, that was a guilty start! What have you been up to, Giddy? Reading my diary or just sneaking a piece of chocolate cake?

GIDDY. Uh ... are those the only choices I get?

CHARLENE. Say, you *are* nervous! Honey, I was only kidding. I'm just tired from bucking all that traffic. Where do all those marathon-spectators *come* from every year! (*Starts down into room, GIDDY trailing uneasily after her*) I swear, the roads must be empty from here to California, judging by the number of cars on the streets of *Boston* today—(*Stops moving as she sees BRET; blinks hard; then:*) Giddy! Who's *that*?

GIDDY. (*With a tiny shrug*) I have no idea! (*Then, gazing in warm adoration upon BRET's slumbering form*) But isn't he *dreamy*?!

CHARLENE. You don't know who he *is*? How did he *get* here?

GIDDY. A very nice policeman brought him. I don't know *how* I'd have managed *alone*!

CHARLENE. Brought him? He couldn't get here under his own power?

GIDDY. Oh, no. He was totally unconscious. Still is, actually.

CHARLENE. I don't understand *any* of this ... Gideon Hollis—where did you *get* this guy?

GIDDY. He was lying in the middle of the street, and he looked *so* handsome and helpless, I couldn't just leave him there—!

CHARLENE. Giddy, have you lost your *mind*? Picking up a strange man— (*Looks from GIDDY to BRET then back at GIDDY and amplifies:*) literally—and bringing him to our apartment—?! (*Looks at BRET again, adds:*) In his *underwear*?!

GIDDY. That's *not* underwear. That's his running-outfit. It's what *everybody* wears.

CHARLENE. Wait. A light's beginning to dawn ... I think. This man was running in the *marathon* today?

GIDDY. And collapsed just short of the finish-line, poor guy. That's what helped me decide.

CHARLENE. (*Warily*) Decide what ...?

GIDDY. That he was just the sort of man I've been trying to meet all my life! I mean, a real *hunk*, you know? Hunks almost *never* come to the *museum*. It's pretty dull there for the kind of men with *muscles* ...

CHARLENE. Look, forget your assistant curator's job for a moment, and backtrack a sentence or two. I want to know what you meant about his collapse helping your decision.

GIDDY. (*Business of removing one coverlet from BRET, putting other on him*) He never finished the race. Everyone else came in, but he didn't.

CHARLENE. (*Realizes GIDDY's explanation is apparently over, so insists:*) And...?

GIDDY. (*Still fussing with coverlet, tossing too-short coverlet onto armchair*) Isn't it *obvious*?

CHARLENE. Not even *slightly!*

GIDDY. (*Gives final pat to coverlet on BRET., turns to face her, explains merrily:*) *Nice* guys finish *last!* (*As CHARLENE does a jaw-drop gape:*) So I just *knew* this guy was Mister Right!

CHARLENE. (*Almost reeling with shock*) Giddy, that is *not* what that expression *means!*

GIDDY. Nonsense! What else *could* it mean?! (*Glances adoringly down on BRET.*) I think I'll call him "Antonio"! Italians are *so* romantic! Would you mind?

CHARLENE. No ... but *he* might! Listen, honey— (*Will toss too-short coverlet onto back of armchair and gently lead GIDDY to sit in armchair, during:*) I'm flattered that you value my opinion, but this setup is *beyond* the realm of Mommy-he-followed-me-home-can-I-*keep*-him!

GIDDY. But he *didn't* follow me. I had him delivered!

CHARLENE. Gideon Hollis—to paraphrase an old maxim—you *can't* just catch a fallen *stud* and put him in your *parlor!*

GIDDY. Then *where?*

CHARLENE. *No*where! "Parlor" isn't the *point!*

GIDDY. Then what is?

CHARLENE. (*Will sit on arm of armchair U of GIDDY, softening her tone*) Listen, my dear sweet knuckleheaded baby, there are *laws* against simply *taking* people. Even *Italian* people! ... Say, how do you *know* if he's an Italian?

GIDDY 'Cause I've always *wanted* one, But Daddy said no. Daddy said no to a *lot* of things

CHARLENE. Honey, what has kidnapping fallen racers got to do with your *father*?

GIDDY. Everything! If it weren't for Daddy, I'd have been in love and married *years* ago! He kept scaring all my boyfriends *off!*

CHARLENE. Chased them out of the house, or what?

GIDDY. Oh, he let them come *in*, he wasn't *that* strict. He even let them take me *out*.

[NOTE: *It's hard to remain corpse-rigid indefinitely; your BRET is free to breathe, move his head to one side or the other, shift an arm, etc., like any unconscious person. He must not distract the audience from the action onstage, of course, in doing so; but he needn't "play dead" during his lengthy sojourn on the sofa. The ladies—unless specified—can mostly ignore his moves, perhaps giving him a brief glance now and then as he shifts, but no more, and then returning to their conversation/business/etc.]*

CHARLENE. So what was the *problem*, then?

GIDDY. The *way* he did it! A guy would show up at the door for a date and Daddy would invite him in—then take full-front and profile *Polaroids* of him—

CHARLENE. Oh, dear.

GIDDY. Then he'd have them produce an I.D., like a driver's license, and check their faces against the picture on the I.D.—

CHARLENE. Oh, my.

GIDDY. Then when we'd leave, Daddy would follow us downstairs, come outside, and take down the license-number of the guy's *car* before we left! He was *only* being protective of me, and I love him for it—but it created an *awful* social strain!

CHARLENE. I can see where it *would*. Ah, but what the heck, that was only on your *first* date with a guy, while he was compiling a *dossier* on him. He *must* have eased off for the *second* date.

GIDDY. (*Quietly, wistfully*) I never *had* a second date.

CHARLENE. (*Almost in tears*) Aw, sweetie—!

GIDDY. My friends called me One-Shot Hollis! Meet a boy, go out, come home, stay there. (*Clutches CHARLENE's hands*) So when this Dreamboat—this potential *Antonio*—this gorgeous hunk of man—just about dropped into my *lap*—well—what else *could* I do but ... follow through!

CHARLENE. But Giddy...my dear friend ... this man may not even turn out to *be* Italian. And he may *resent* being abducted, even by a girl as cute as you. And, most important of all, there are *laws* against finding unconscious people and carrying them off!

GIDDY. Don't be ridiculous. Ambulance drivers do it every day!

CHARLENE. Giddy, that's their *job!* They're *licensed* to do it!

GIDDY. (*Shrugs*) Then it *can't* be against the law! You can't get a license to *break* the law, can you?

CHARLENE. (*Slightly swamped by this eerie logic*) Well—uh—*no*, of *course* you can't, but—how can I explain it? ... There are *some* occasions ... some very *particular* circumstances, mind you ... when something that's *usually* against the law ... um ... *isn't* against the law! Like—like—?

GIDDY. Like crossing against the light when a street gang's after you?

CHARLENE. Uh—right! That's a somewhat *cockeyed* example, but exactly right!

GIDDY. Then what *law* have I broken? When a man's lying senseless in the middle of a street you can't just *leave* him there, can you?

CHARLENE. (*Losing ground*) Well—no—but— bringing him to your *apartment*—!

GIDDY. (*With the logic of the sweetly insane*) I suppose I should have plunked him down on the *curb?* Left him sprawled on the *sidewalk?* Leaned him up against a *lamppost?*

CHARLENE. Well—*no*—but—!

GIDDY. And we live *only* two blocks *away* from there, Charlene. So why shouldn't he regain consciousness on a nice soft *sofa?* Seems the *least* I could do for him.

CHARLENE. Wait. Let me think. I can't quite put my finger on it, but—there's *got* to be a flaw in your logic *someplace* ... I mean—there are *laws!*

GIDDY. Nonsense. If I was doing anything illegal would that *policeman* have helped me? In broad daylight?

CHARLENE. (*Very little wind left in her sails*) Huh. That *is* a stumper. Say—how did that policeman *get* into the act, anyhow? You must have used up every *kilowatt* of charm to coax him into toting a man *this* size all the way from Copley Square!

GIDDY. (*Preening a bit, offhandedly*) Didn't *have* to charm him. I simply told him Dreamboat was my *husband!*

CHARLENE. (*Jumps to her feet, says dramatically:*) AHA! (*GIDDY winces at the sudden blast*) I *knew* there was a flaw someplace! (*Points accusatory finger*) *You* told a *lie* to a *policeman!*

GIDDY. (*Unfazed, shrugs as if dismissing the topic*) Oh, *that!*

CHARLENE. (*With frustration*) Yes! That!

GIDDY. But policemen are *used* to being lied to, Charlene! (*Enumerating by example:*) "I thought the speed limit was *forty!*" ... "*What* no-left-turn sign?" ... "I didn't *hear* you whistle."

CHARLENE. Giddy, those are *misdemeanor* lies! *We* are discussing a potential *felony!*

GIDDY. But felons lie more than *anybody*, Charlene!

CHARLENE. And go to *jail* for it! Gideon, can't you get it through your pretty head that if that policeman should find out that this man *isn't* your husband—

GIDDY. (*Calmly*) He won't do a thing.

CHARLENE. (*Blinks*) He won't? Why won't he?

GIDDY. Because he *helped* me get this man *up* here, Charlene.

CHARLENE. But—

GIDDY. That makes him an accessory!

CHARLENE. But—

GIDDY. He'd lose his *job* if he snitched on me!

CHARLENE. (*Slowly sits again on chair arm; then:*) Hold it. Let me mull that over. It *sounds* plausible, but there must be *something* you're overlooking!

GIDDY. Nothing *I* can think of ...

CHARLENE. (*Jumps to her feet again*) AHA! (*GIDDY winces again*)

GIDDY. I wish you'd stop *shouting* that, Charlene.

CHARLENE. (*Patiently*) Giddy, when *aha*-time arrives, a person can't *whisper* it—and *aha*-time is definitely *here,* baby!

GIDDY. But why? Just what *is* it you think I'm overlooking?

CHARLENE. (*Points to BRET.*) Dreamboat! That's what! He must belong to somebody—by now they'll be out looking for him—and if they report him missing—!

GIDDY. Nothing will happen. When you report a missing person the police don't do anything about it for twenty-four hours. It's the law!

CHARLENE. (*Turns palms up, looks ceilingward*) *Now* she turns law-abiding!

GIDDY. (*Rises from chair, stand at L end of sofa gazing upon BRET.*) A lot can *happen* in twenty-four hours ...

CHARLENE. Giddy, a lot can happen in *five minutes* if this man awakens in a strange apartment in his *underwear*!

GIDDY. I *put* a *coverlet* over him! ... And *I* don't think our apartment's so strange!

CHARLENE. (*Gently*) Yes it is. *You* live here.

GIDDY. Charlene. Be fair. If I found a *penny* in the street and brought it home, nobody would care.

CHARLENE. Giddy—

GIDDY. If I found a *kitten* in the street and brought it home, nobody would care.

CHARLENE. *Giddy*—

GIDDY. If I found a *horsie* in the street—

CHARLENE. *WHOA! No way* could you bring a *horse* into this apartment building!

GIDDY. But I *didn't*—I brought a *man*! *Lots* of girls bring men to their apartments!

CHARLENE. *Not* unconscious and undressed!

GIDDY. Are you sure...?

CHARLENE. (*Abashed*) Well, no, but— (*Recovers her mind*) Wait a minute, we're *way* off the subject! This has nothing to do with romance!

GIDDY. It has *everything* to do with romance!

CHARLENE. How do you figure?

GIDDY. I've got it all planned. After awhile, he'll stir ... his eyelashes will flutter ... he'll pop them open—

CHARLENE. His *eyelashes?*!

GIDDY. His *eyes*! You know what I mean!

CHARLENE. Sorry. Pray continue ...

GIDDY. He'll see me ... he'll ask how he got here ...

CHARLENE. *That* part of the fantasy I concur with!

GIDDY. And I'll tell him. And he'll be grateful. And gratitude will turn to friendship. And friendship will turn to love. And then he'll take me in his arms and—

CHARLENE. Kiddo, you're asking an awful *lot* of the next twenty-four *hours*!

GIDDY. Am not. It's *April*, Charlene—springtime! And in the spring a young man's fancy—

CHARLENE. The poet was *not* writing about *kidnap* victims! And that's what this man *is*! Honey, you can't just go out on the street and *take* a man because you like his *looks*!

GIDDY. "Can't"? Aren't you overlooking the obvious? I already *did*! And here he is! And if everything works out, someday soon I'll be able to say, "I take this man—"

CHARLENE. (*Dryly*) "—as my lawful wedded hostage!"

GIDDY. He is *not* a hostage!

CHARLENE. Will you let him *go* if he doesn't marry you?

GIDDY. Well ...

CHARLENE. *See*?! So when you hold a person anywhere against his will—

[NOTE: *From this point of the act, it will start to get DARK outside the window, reaching full darkness just before BRET has his telephone call scene; the shift should be slow and unobtrusive, so that the audience will (probably) not notice till the characters do.*]

GIDDY. *You* keep patients in the *hospital* against their will all the *time*! Would you call *them* hostages?

CHARLENE. Yes.

GIDDY. (*Struggling to win this semantic debate*) But you don't hold them for *ransom*, do you?!

CHARLENE. What do you call the *hospital bill?*! They *pay*—or they *stay!*

GIDDY. Some angel-of-mercy *you* are! People in the medical field should be there for love of humanity, not just to make *money!*

CHARLENE. That's going to be news to the American Medical Association!

GIDDY. (*Reacts as BRET stirs slightly and mumbles in his sleep*) Lower your voice, you're waking him up!

CHARLENE. I thought you *wanted* him to wake up.

GIDDY. (*Starts for bedroom, toting that too-small coverlet*) Not till I fix my face and put on a prettier dress! And I'd prefer to be *alone* with him—

CHARLENE. But *think*—(*While GIDDY exits to bedroom with coverlet*) Are you sure you *want* to be alone with him? What if he's a maniac, or a sadist, or a burglar, or—

GIDDY. (*Off*) You don't have to leave the *apartment,* Charlene; just—go into the bedroom and read a book or something.

CHARLENE. I'd *much* rather listen at the door! ... Say, that just conjured up *another* merry little thought in my mind: What if he doesn't speak *English?* A lot of people *don't,* these days!

GIDDY. (*Off*) I'll *teach* him to speak it!

CHARLENE. In twenty-four hours?

GIDDY. (*Off*) You know—that just made me *think* of something! (*Re-enters*)

CHARLENE. There's always a first time.

GIDDY. (*Ignoring this*) It's been almost *two hours* since I found him! Shouldn't he be *awake* by now ...?

CHARLENE. It *is* a pretty long time for a simple *nap* ... (*Moves to him, takes his pulse, while GIDDY hovers just U of sofa*) His *pulse* seems fairly normal, slow and steady. I'd better smell his breath!

GIDDY. Charlene, I'm *sure* he's not an alcoholic!

CHARLENE. Why?

GIDDY. I've seen them in the movies. They always need a shave.

CHARLENE. Not *female* alcoholics. Well, not *all* of them. (*Starts sniffing his breath*)

GIDDY. What are you *doing*, then?

CHARLENE. Checking for ketosis. The man *might* be in a diabetic *coma*! Ketosis is the characteristic smell on a diabetic's breath. (*Suddenly reacts to her sniffing, pulls away*) Pee-yoooo!

GIDDY. Ketosis?

CHARLENE. I'm not sure. It's certainly not *normal* breath. But ketosis is supposed to have a sweet, fruity sort of smell—if *this* is it, that fruit is *rotten!*

GIDDY. Maybe he forgot to brush after his last meal?

CHARLENE. (*Comes around sofa to flank GIDDY*) I doubt it. Unless his last meal was rotten fruit!

GIDDY. Oh, dear, I *would* get a hunk with halitosis!

CHARLENE. No, it's not that, either. I'm not sure *what* it is! I wish I knew more about physical exhaustion. Maybe this happens when a runner hits The Wall.

GIDDY. Can't be. He was right in the middle of Copley Square.

CHARLENE. Honey, "The Wall" is a phrase coined by runners—it means an almost-tangible *barrier* they run up against when their legs won't carry them any farther.

GIDDY. And it makes their *breath* smell bad?

CHARLENE. For all *I* know! I wish I'd paid better attention at nursing school. (*Abruptly starts for phone*) We'll have to check with his family. He *might* be in need of some medication. You don't want a *dead* hostage on your hands! (*Picks up phone*) What's his number?

GIDDY. How should *I* know? I've never *phoned* him.

CHARLENE. Not his telephone number, his registration number—you know, that thing all the marathon-runners have on their backs. You can't miss it, it's half-a-foot square!

GIDDY. But he didn't *have* a number when I found him. Maybe it fell off during the race.

(*Room-LIGHTING is down to about three-quarters by now*)

CHARLENE. Damn. (*Hangs up phone*) I *was* going to call the marathon committee and get a quick I.D. *that* way. Hell, I don't know *what* to do *now*! How *can* we reach his family?

GIDDY. We can't. So maybe we'd better call a doctor, huh?

CHARLENE. On Patriot's Day? Don't be ridiculous. They're all out celebrating the race.

GIDDY. How about someone on duty, from *your* hospital?

CHARLENE. On a holiday? Sorry, Giddy. Skeleton staff only—and they don't make house calls.

GIDDY. (*Leans over sofa back, gently strokes BRET's hair*) Well, at least he's not going to die in the *street*.

CHARLENE. With a pulse as strong as his, he's not going to die at *all*! But *why* doesn't he wake *up*?

GIDDY. (*With sudden elation*) Maybe he's under a *spell*! *You* know, like Sleeping Beauty! And all he needs to awaken him is—

CHARLENE. Giddy! You are *not* going to *kiss* this man! It wouldn't help a bit!

GIDDY. (*Abashed*) It couldn't *hurt* ...

CHARLENE. Play by the rules, kid. How would *you* feel if *you* were lying unconscious and a handsome *man* started to—(*Sees the growing elation on GIDDY's face, stops example, tries again:*) Let me put it another way:

There are *two* very good reasons why you are not going to kiss this unconscious man!

GIDDY. *What* reasons?

CHARLENE. Number One, taking romantic advantage of the comatose is *very* poor sportsmanship!

GIDDY. (*This hits home, but she wistfully inquires:*) And Number *Two*—?

CHARLENE. His *breath* would knock you on your *keester*!

GIDDY. (*Reluctantly*) Well, if you put it *that* way ...

CHARLENE. (*Musing hard*) I *wish* I could place that *odor* ... ghastly as it is, there's something *familiar* about it ... a kind of *chemical* odor that I know I should *recognize*. ... If I could *only*—? (*Shifts gears*) We're wasting time. If we were a little *stronger*, I'd say we take the *brute* approach to revival—standing him up and *walking* him.

GIDDY. If we *tried* hard enough, I'm sure the two of us could *carry* him ...

(*Room-LIGHTING is down to about two-thirds by now*)

CHARLENE. Like a sack of potatoes, *sure*, but he has to be walked *upright*, getting those *legs* moving, pumping the blood back to his *brain*! (*Moves to lamp*)

GIDDY. Maybe that *policeman* can help us walk him when he comes back!

CHARLENE. (*Has noticed dimming of room and turns on lamp [LIGHTS UP FULL] just as GIDDY's remark registers, and she reacts:*) Back *here*? What *for*?

GIDDY. To double-check on Dreamboat. He said he'd be back about *nine*.

CHARLENE. And you *agreed*?

GIDDY. What *else* could I do? He didn't think Dreamboat should be left on the sofa.

CHARLENE. So why didn't you have him stash Dreamboat in the *bedroom*?

GIDDY. What if *you* were in there? How could I *explain* you?

CHARLENE. Say I'm the cleaning-lady!

GIDDY. And if you were in the *shower*?

CHARLENE. Say I was a *sweaty* cleaning-lady! I'd been scrubbing floors all day and—(*Realizes*) What am I saying?! Good grief, I'm starting to think like *you!* (*KNOCK at door; CHARLENE. panics*) Who's that knocking at our door?

GIDDY. (*Sing-songs merrily:*) It's *Bar*nacle *Bill* the *saiiii*-lor!

CHARLENE. *Who*?

GIDDY. That's the *answer* to who's knocking at the door. In an old song my late grandmother used to sing to me.

CHARLENE. We'll both be *joining* your late grandmother if it's that *cop* out there!

GIDDY. But it's nowhere *near* nine o'clock.

CHARLENE. (*Final three words loud enough to be heard through door:*) Then *who is it*?

DEX. (*Off*) It's Dex, honey!

[NOTE: *They'll address each other in furtive tones, DEX in normal*]

CHARLENE. (*To GIDDY*) Oh, no! My fiance! And me with a half-naked man!

GIDDY. (*To CHARLENE.*) You, *too*?! (*KNOCK repeats; CHARLENE rushes up, stops just at door*)

CHARLENE. *Damn it, hold your horses!* (*Then, belatedly, in more dulcet tones, adds:*) ... darling.

DEX. (*Off*) I'd *like* to come *in* ...

CHARLENE. *Why*?

DEX. (*Off*) Well, for one thing—we have a *dinner-date!*

CHARLENE. We *do*?! (*To GIDDY, in shock*) We have a *dinner*-date!

GIDDY. (*In shock*) Tonight?

CHARLENE. (*Nods unhappily*) Apparently! (*To DEX:*) Honey, are you *sure*?

DEX. (*Off*) Look, can I come *in* while we discuss this?

GIDDY/CHARLENE. *NO!*

DEX. (*Off*) Why the hell *not*?

GIDDY. (*Improvising inanely*) We have no *clothes* on!

DEX. (*Off, instantly, in a gleefully squeaky high voice of anticipation [kidding]*) Please-can-I-come-in?!

CHARLENE. (*Almost doubles up with a snort of laughter*) You clown! (*By reflex, reaches for doorknob*)

GIDDY. (*Frantically flailing a finger at BRET.*) Charleeeeen—!

CHARLENE. (*Remembers, recovers former mood; to DEX:*) Look—*Give* us just a second, *will*, you, honey—? (*Signals GIDDY, and BOTH rush down to sofa, GIDDY taking BRET's wrists, CHARLENE taking his ankles, and they tote him awkwardly around sofa and toward bedroom [coverlet dangling from him], during:*)

DEX. (*Off*) What's the problem? Are you two smoking *pot* or something?

GIDDY. (*Grunting with towing-effort, with sad sincerity*) I *wish!*

DEX. (*Off*) You *what?*

CHARLENE. She's *kidding*, honey! We'll just be a few more seconds! (*To GIDDY before she can quite collide with D door jamb*) Watch the wall!

GIDDY. Oops! Thanks! (*They will vanish into bedroom with BRET during:*)

DEX. (*Off*) What's going *on* in there? You sound like you're moving furniture!

(Next bits of the gals' speeches may be OFF or ON, depending on how fast they can lug BRET out of view and return to foyer area)

GIDDY. (*Inspired*) Yes! That's it! We're moving furniture!

DEX. (*Off*) Don't you want some *help?*

CHARLENE. We want the new arrangement to be a *surprise!*

DEX. (*Off*) *Why?*

GIDDY. For Patriot's Day!

DEX. (*Off*) I don't *get* it! *Why* surprise me because it's Patriot's Day?

CHARLENE. You're a *patriot*, aren't you?! (*They are both back in foyer now, puffing and smoothing their dresses and fluffing their hair, etc., prior to admitting him*)

DEX. (*Off*) Damn it, Charlene, are you going to open this door or aren't you?!

GIDDY. He sounds *mad.*

DEX. (*Off*) He *is* mad!

CHARLENE. (*Process of opening door, during:*) Honey, you were *only* out there a few minutes!

(DEXTER CLAYTON enters; he is a nice-looking young man in a suit and tie, carrying a tall-and-narrow brown bag)

DEX. Yes, but *why?*

CHARLENE. (*Leading him D of foyer while GIDDY closes door*) Now-now, don't be a grouchy old bear! We just weren't quite *ready* for visitors!

DEX. (*Glances around in puzzlement*) I thought you were rearranging the *furniture*—?

GIDDY. The *bedroom* furniture!

DEX. (*To CHARLENE..*) You were going to surprise me in the *bedroom*?

CHARLENE. (*As if shocked*) Dexter Clayton, *shame* on you!

DEX. You know damn well what I meant! What has been going *on* in here, you two?! You'd think you were hiding a *man*!

(*BOTH instantly go into high-pitched laughter; then*:)

GIDDY. Now *why* would we do a thing like *that*?

DEX. (*Logically, with a shrug*) So I wouldn't *find* him here, I suppose. That's the *usual* reason for hiding men.

CHARLENE. (*Turns him from GIDDY, takes him warmly in her arms*) But darling, I have *nothing* to hide from *you*—! (*Behind his back, GIDDY makes frantic motions, pointing toward bedroom, and then indicating that CHARLENE should get DEX out of the place, fast; CHARLENE catches her drift, and, still in warm embrace, just before DEX's approaching lips can connect with hers, shoves him away and starts merrily toward foyer, on*:) Well, let's get *going*!

DEX. Going? Going *where*? You invited me to *dinner*...?!

GIDDY/CHARLENE. (*In dual shock*) HERE?!

DEX. (*Extends bag*) I don't *usually* bring a bottle of wine to drink in a *cab*!

CHARLENE. (*Fingertips to temples, remembering aloud*:) I *knew* there was something I had to do after I got home from work: *Shopping*!

DEX. You mean you *didn't*?

CHARLENE. I got ... sort of ... *involved*, and—well—? (*Sags sorrowfully*)

GIDDY. (*Inspired*) Say! Why don't you take her *out* to dinner?! A nice restaurant—candlelight—wine—!

DEX. On Patriot's Day?! There won't be an available table anywhere in town! They book them *months* in advance!

CHARLENE. He's right, Giddy, they *do*...! But Dex, I don't think we have anything to eat *here* but *Wheaties*!

DEX. If you had a *normal* job, you'd have today *off*, and could have been *through* with your shopping!

CHARLENE. Is it *my* fault hospitals don't shut down for holidays?!

GIDDY. (*Peacemaker*) Now-now, you two, don't fight—(*Then glances toward bedroom and suddenly changes attitude*) Wait. I changed my mind. *Do* fight! (*Like a director organizing a scene:*) Charlene, *you* slap his face, then—Dex—*you* break the engagement, and, Charlene, *you* say you never want to see him again as long as you live, and *you*, Dex, go out and slam the door after you, and— (*Stops; sees the two of them are just standing and staring at her as if she'd gone loony; she thinks a second, then says weakly:*) You can *always* kiss-and-make-up *tomorrow* ... (*When they still continue to stare at her, she says, elatedly:*) Shopping! Or course! You can do your shopping *now*!

CHARLENE. (*With similar elation*) Yes! That's *it!* It's *perfect*! We can shop for—oh—hours, maybe!

DEX. "We"? You're going to leave me here alone?

GIDDY. (*Exasperated*) *No*, stupid, *you* and *Charlene* do the shopping!

DEX. *Both* of us?

CHARLENE. (*Takes his arm, turns on the kilowatts*) You can pick out all your favorite *foods*—

GIDDY. Yeah, all that weird stuff that *men* like so much—smoked oysters, beef jerky, beer nuts—!

DEX. (*With queasy uncertainty*) That'd make a *hell* of a meal—!

CHARLENE. (*As though he'd shown wild enthusiasm, links arms with him on:*) *Wouldn't* it, though? I'm salivating *already!* (*Nearly yanks him off his feet on:*) C'mon! (*Has him half-towed to foyer before:*)

DEX. (*Pulls free*) *Wait* a minute! I'm *not* going down the sidewalk looking like a *wino!* (*Hands bagged wine to GIDDY*)

GIDDY. (*Looks from him to bag*) Why not? You came *up* the sidewalk looking like a wino—?!

CHARLENE. (*Grabs his arm again*) But I love you *anyhow!* C'mon, before the *stores* close!

DEX. (*Disengages his arm in mid-tow*) Can the stores wait another *two minutes*—?

GIDDY. What *for?*

DEX. (*Moving toward bedroom*) I have to use the *bathroom*—! (*This time* both *women lurch to grab him by either arm, on:*)

GIDDY/CHARLENE. You *can't!*

DEX. But I *have* to! (*Resists [not quite successfully] their mutual tow toward foyer*) I mean, *really* have to! *Bad!*

CHARLENE. There's a gas station on the corner!

DEX. Why can't I use *this* bathroom?

GIDDY. (*Inspired*) It's being *fixed!*

DEX. (*Pulls free of both grasps just as CHARLENE gets front door open*) "Fixed"?

GIDDY. They had to take it back to the shop!

DEX. The *bathroom*?!

CHARLENE. The *pipes!*

GIDDY. They were all corroded!

CHARLENE. They have to bring new ones!

GIDDY. The bathroom can't be used at all!

DEX. Not even for—?

CHARLENE. Not till tomorrow.

GIDDY. We couldn't get them to deliver the new pipes on a holiday.

DEX. Say—if the bathroom's out of commission—what—what do *you* two do if—if—?

GIDDY. Grit our teeth and smile!

DEX. That's *crazy*!

GIDDY. (*Shrugs and says explanatorily:*) *I'm* crazy!

CHARLENE. You can say *that* again! (*Grabs DEX's arm*) C'*mon*, already!

DEX. (*Resisting.*) But—?!

GIDDY. (*Tosses bagged wine onto sofa, grabs DEX's other arm*) Dex, you'll never *make* it to the gas station! (*Both women drag him out door and out of sight, on:*)

DEX. I won't if you don't stop *shaking* me...!

(*They are gone; there is a two-second silence; outside the window, hazily visible through the closed-but-gauzy window curtains, it is now as dark as it's going to get, though we can see a random assortment of bright rectangles which are the windows of the townhouses on the opposite side of the street; after those two seconds, there appear two sets of four fingers, about a foot apart, on the D edge of the door jamb of the exit to the bedroom; then the hair, then the forehead, then the eyes, and finally the entire face of BRET appear between those fingers; he looks a bit punchy and not a little uneasy; seeing no one, he eases himself into the room and straightens up and moves a few steps into the room, staring about in bewilderment; he is still in tank-top, shorts, shoes, socks and nothing else; moving as quietly as possible, he gets to still-open door and peeks out and down the hall; then he comes down into the room and peeks carefully off into the kitchen; he seems abruptly relieved, heaves a slight sigh, then hurries to telephone, grabs up receiver, dials a number quickly, then stands against D side of desk, facing out front,*

*right hand holding receiver to his ear; a brief pause;
then:)*

BRET. *(On phone, his voice at first frantic)* Police? ...
I've been kidnapped! ... *(Incredulously)* Of *course* it's an
emergency! ... But I don't *know* the number of the local
police station, that's why I dialed *nine-one-one*! I don't even
know where I *am*! ... *(Incredulity mingling with
annoyance)* Of *course* I left the scene of the crime! Kidnap-
victims *always* leave the scene of the crime! ... It *can't* be
illegal! How could a victim *not* leave with his kidnappers?
... *(Patiently, but getting a little grim)* I *know* it's my duty
to try and get away—that's what I'm doing *now*! ... *(Anger
starting to show)* Damn it, will you *stop* calling it the
"alleged" crime! It *happened*! ...Where? In Copley Square,
I guess. That's the *last* place I can remember being ... *(A
little calmer)* Here? I guess it must be the *kidnappers'*
apartment ... No, I *didn't* see them, there's nobody here ...
(Nods at whatever phonee is saying) Yeah, that *is* pretty
lax of them, I guess ... *(Angry)* No, this is *not* a crank
call!...Of *course* I sound cranky—I *am* cranky! ... Look, all
I know is that I'm in a strange woman's apartment in my
underwear!... *(Exasperated)* Don't say *congratulations*, I
want to get *out* of here! ... *(With thinning patience)* I'd
love to come downtown and sign a complaint, but how do
I *get* downtown?! ... *(Explodes)* I'm *not* asking for
directions! I mean, how can I get there in my *underwear?* ...
Yes, there are clothes in the closet, but they're all *dresses*!
That's how I knew this was a *woman's* apartment! ... *(With
an uneasy look behind him toward bedroom, almost to
himself:)* At least, I *hope* it is! ... *(Concentrating on call
again)* A what—? Window? ... *(Looks U again, brightens)*
Hey, yeah, there *is*! Hang on a second—! *(Sets down
phone, goes to window, opens curtains a crack at center,
shifts his head left-and-right to scan the outside street, then*

returns to phone somewhat dejectedly, picks it up again, and:) No dice. Too dark out to read the street-sign on the corner, so I *still* don't know where I am! ... Nope. Only thing I could see is an old lady in the townhouse across the street, scanning the neighborhood with a pair of binoculars—hey, hang on a second, that just gave me an idea! ... *(Sets down phone, rushes to window, holds curtains wide-apart with both hands and does a little dance, while caroling provocatively:)* Woo-woo! Woo-woo! Woo-woo! *(Stares out a moment longer, nods in satisfaction, drops the curtains back into place, hurries and gets back on phone)* It worked! ... Well, I did a kind of dance in the window, she saw me, and she went for her phone like greased lightning! Now all you have to do is wait for her call to come through, and she'll tell the address where she saw me, and you can send a *rescue*-wagon for me! ... Sure I'll wait! ... *(Stands there, whistling idly, tapping one foot in time to tune; then:)* What? ... Are you *sure*? ... Oh boy, I hope she didn't have *heart*-failure before she could put the call *through*! Let me check—! *(Downs phone, rushes to window, peeks out; his shoulders sag; he turns and moves wearily back to phone, picks it up, and:)* Now there are *five* old ladies with binoculars! *(Abruptly listens toward front doorway, reacts)* Someone's coming! I'll call you back! *(Hangs up, looks around in panic, then rushes into kitchen; a moment later, GIDDY re-enters from hall, shuts door, comes down into room)*

GIDDY. *(Sees wine bag on sofa)* Oops, can't leave *you* there! *(Merrily proceeds to desk, takes wine bottle from bag, sets it on desk, crumples bag into a ball and drops it into the wastebasket there; she is facing D enough so that BRET can come out of kitchen unnoticed U of her, tiptoe close behind her, and jab her in the back, on:)*

BRET. *Freeze,* Turkey! *(She automatically starts to turn around to her left, stopping when she is facing directly L, so that BRET has to scurry a bit downstage to remain out-of-view* behind *her; this is so, since BOTH are now in profile to us, we can see that BRET's "weapon" is a large curving* banana, *the shorter end of its curve serving as the "pistol butt" in his grip, the tip of the longer end serving as the "mouth of the gunbarrel" against her back; as she moves—and he countermoves—he shouts in desperation [since she must not see that "weapon"]:*) Don't turn around!

GIDDY. (*Terrified*) Why not?

BRET. I'll blow you away, *that's* why not!

GIDDY. But—how did you get *in* here—what do you *want*—?!

BRET. I want you to stand there with your hands up!

GIDDY. *Forever?*

BRET. Of course not! You're going to telephone the police!

GIDDY. What makes you think *that?*

BRET. That wasn't a prediction, it was an order!

GIDDY. Who do you think you *are,* coming in here and telling people what to do?!

BRET. *I'll* tell you who I am! I'm— (*He pauses for about three seconds, the banana angling down a bit, then:*) I'm ... (*Another three seconds, the banana now pointing floorward, his stance a bit limp with amazement as he realizes aloud:*) I don't *know* who I am!

GIDDY. (*Turns, sees who's been holding her at "gunpoint," and carols:*) Antonio! (*Flings her arms about him, her right cheek against his chest, her eyes closed, her smile rapturous*)

BRET. (*Out front, as aghast as if she'd called him a leper*) I'm *Italian*?!

GIDDY. (*Pulls free, clasps her hands to her breast in delight, replies as if his question had been a declaration*) Oh, I *knew* it! I just *knew* it! (*Embraces him again as before*) Carissima! [kah-REES-see-mah]

BRET. (*By reflex, corrects the gender of her endearment:*) "Carissim*o*"! [kah-rees-see-MOH]

GIDDY. Sorry. *Carissimo*! (*Looks up at him*) Your turn.

BRET. (*Pushes her away—but not too forcefully; he's beginning to like what he sees—on:*) I am *not* swapping endearments! I was simply changing you to the proper *gender!*

GIDDY. (*Shies slightly back, palms crisscrossed upon her chest*) You were *what?*

BRET. Not your *torso*, your *grammar!*

GIDDY. Well, *that's* a relief! (*Takes a step toward him to re-embrace him, but:*)

BRET. (*Whips up banana gun-like again*) Hold it right there!

GIDDY. (*Raises her hands as if he* did *have a weapon*) I'm holding, I'm holding!

BRET. What *is* this place? Where *am* I? *Why* am I here?

GIDDY. (*Flatly incredulous, half-dropping her hands*) You want to discuss *philosophy?*

BRET. (*Re those dropping hands*) *No* you don't! (*Re-threatens with banana, she re-raises hands*) Now look, lady ... please ... I need some answers!

GIDDY. (*Sincerely, even if it is a dopey interpretation of his remark*) You're cramming for your finals?

BRET. I want to know what I'm *doing* here!

GIDDY. (*Shrugs*) You're shouting and threatening, can't you tell?

BRET. Listen, let's take this thing in easy stages. First off—where are my clothes?

GIDDY. How should *I* know? That's all I've ever *seen* you in!

BRET. I *arrived* here like this?

GIDDY. (*Drops her hands, now curled into fists, onto her hips, arms akimbo*) What do *you* think?! I certainly didn't *strip* you! What do you think I *am*?

BRET. A kidnapper!

GIDDY. Now, *really*, Antonio, do I *look* like a kidnapper?

BRET. (*Sincerely*) I don't *know*—I've never been *kidnapped* before ...

GIDDY. (*Takes half-step toward him*) Look, why don't you put down that banana, and—

BRET. (*Takes backstep, leveling "weapon" at her*) Careful! I know how to *use* this! (*Realizes, sags, lowers "weapon"*) Oh. You *knew* it was a banana!

GIDDY. (*Honestly*) Well, not at *first*, to be honest about it. Mostly I saw *you*, and your menacing *attitude*, and that you were holding *something*— (*Shrugs*)—but I don't *stay* stupid for long! (*Suddenly laughs*)

BRET. What's so funny?

GIDDY. I was just thinking—if my *friends* came back while you were holding me at bay— I probably would have shouted, "Watch *out*! He's got a *banana*!" (*BOTH laugh; then, abruptly:*)

BRET. (*Suddenly realizes*) Your *friends*! Then this *is* a hideout! You were just *playing* with me! Stalling for time—*pretending* to be a numbskull!

GIDDY. (*Insulted*) I was *not* pretending! ... Wait, let me re-phrase that— (*But she has no opportunity, because at this moment CHARLENE and DEX enter from hall [no key-using this time; let's assume the door was left unlocked], DEX encumbered with two large bags of groceries in his arms; they see the twosome by desk, and stop in divergent dismays*)

DEX. Who the hell is *that* guy?

BRET. (*Bewildered, but unafraid, since they certainly aren't menacing to see*) My name's Antonio!

CHARLENE. (*To GIDDY*) It *is*?! ... Hi there, Antonio! I'm Charlene Lockwood. And this is Dexter Clayton. Dex—Antonio.

DEX. (*Thrusts both bags into CHARLENE's arms, looking pugnacious*) I don't care what his *name* is, I want to know what he's doing in my fiancée's apartment *dressed* like that!

CHARLENE. (*Dryly*) He means *undressed* like that.

BRET. (*To GIDDY*) You're his *fiancée*?

GIDDY. (*Brightening, seeing his tinge of unhappiness*) Would it *matter* to you?

DEX. (*Starting down toward BRET.*) Damn it, fella, I want some *answers*, and *fast!*

CHARLENE. (*Can't let fist fight start, shouts desperately:*) WAIT!

DEX. (*Looks her way*) Why?

CHARLENE. (*Stalling.*) There's a *reason* this man is here!

DEX. *What* reason?

CHARLENE. (*Inspired*) He's the *plumber!*

DEX. (*Whirls to BRET, clasps him elatedly by upper arms*) The *bathroom's* fixed?!

GIDDY. (*Catching CHARLENE's ploy*) And *everything* flushes!

DEX. (*Bolting for bedroom exit*) Excuse me!

GIDDY. (*Waits till he's gone; then, to CHARLENE., already knowing the answer:*) The gas station was closed?

CHARLENE. (*Nods*) *Boston* pump-jockeys are *patriots!* (*Starts toward BRET and GIDDY with groceries*) We're lucky Dexter's bladder just overruled his brains! (*Re BRET, to GIDDY*) Now, what about—

GIDDY. (*Afraid CHARLENE will say The Wrong Thing, says quickly to BRET:*) Listen, either *peel* that or put it *back!*

BRET. (*Looks at banana he still grasps*) Oh. Sorry. Forgot I had it. (*BRET exits to kitchen; CHARLENE and GIDDY* immediately *converge DC, speaking as super-fast and* sotto voce *as they can manage:*)

CHARLENE. Giddy, what is going on?!

GIDDY. (*Swooningly*) I've got him eating out of my hand!

CHARLENE. Eating *what*, that *banana*?

GIDDY. (*Since Time Is Of The Essence*) *Forget* the banana!

CHARLENE. (*With kitchenward glance*) It won't be easy...! (*Then, to GIDDY:*) I *still* can't believe your hostage *is* named "Antonio"!

GIDDY. Oh, *I* named him that!

CHARLENE. And he *let* you?!

GIDDY. Well, he can't remember his *own* name, so I thought I'd do him a *favor*!

CHARLENE. (*Almost at the end of her rope*) He'll remember it *some* day!

GIDDY. (*Dismissing this airily*) By *then* we could have *kids*!

CHARLENE. Giddy, this situation is getting out of hand—to put it *mildly!* Grabbing up a total stranger and toting him off—

GIDDY. (*Pleads wistfully*) But don't you remember Dirk Winston?

CHARLENE. *Who?*

GIDDY. The movie actor in Jean Kerr's play *Mary, Mary*—when Bob grabs Mary, Dirk laments not taking Cecil B. DeMille's advice about women: If you *want* her, you don't argue about it, you just pick her up and *take* her!

CHARLENE. That's fine advice for *theatre* people, but *Cecil* didn't live in *Boston*! And this is *not* a woman, it's a *man*!

GIDDY. (*Defensively*) What does *sex* matter?!

CHARLENE. (*Appalled at such emotional apathy*) Bite your tongue!

GIDDY. I mean when it comes to *abducting* people!

CHARLENE. It's a *macho*-thing with men! A lady simply *swoons* with delight when a hulking brute carries her off, but a *man* does *not* enjoy arriving back at camp slung across the pommel of a *girl's* saddle!

GIDDY. The *Amazons* did it all the time!

CHARLENE. Yeah, and their tribe is now *extinct*!

GIDDY. Now, now, everything will be fine, just fine. We'll have a nice dinner, and—

CHARLENE. With *"Antonio"*?! How do I explain to *Dex* why we've invited the *plumber* to dinner?!

GIDDY. Well, it would be very *democratic* of us—and after all, this is *Boston*—!

CHARLENE. Giddy, even *Bostonian* plumbers don't go out dining in their *underwear*! ... I hope.

GIDDY. (*Alert*) They're coming back! Relax! I'll think of something!

CHARLENE. That's what I'm *afraid* of! (*Then she assumes a nonchalant attitude as DEX and BRET re-enter room, and heads for kitchen, fast, on:*) I guess *I'll* just put these *groceries* away! (*To GIDDY, in final* sotto voce *aside:*) Away from Ground Zero! (*But then DEX comes scowlingly down toward BRET, and CHARLENE pauses just short of exit to kitchen,* very *apprehsive, during:*)

DEX. Now, *listen*, fella—!

BRET. (*Turns, is almost nose-to-nose with him as he asks:*) What—?

DEX. (*Reacts to BRET's breath*) Yuccch! (*Hand over nose-and-mouth, turns, lurches a few feet away*)

BRET. (*Bewildered, to GIDDY:*) What *happened*?

GIDDY. (*As in TV commercial, places hand fondly on his shoulder, says:*) Honey ... *maybe* it's your *breath*...!

BRET. (*Reacts, frowns, exhales into cupped palm, sniffs palm, and reels*) *Wow,* is it *ever! What* have I been *eating?*

GIDDY. (*Soothingly*) Why don't you go brush! Your toothbrush is in the bathroom drawer.

BRET. (*Amazed*) It *is?*

CHARLENE. (*Leaning helplessly against D doorjamb of kitchen, out front:*) The bright blue one with the teeny rubber spike on the handle.

BRET. (*Too breath-embarrassed to puzzle matters out at the moment*) Maybe I'd *better!* (*Exits to bedroom, fast, on:*) Excuse me!

DEX. (*Has finally recovered, moves almost ominously toward CHARLENE*) Why is that man's toothbrush in your *bathroom?!*

GIDDY. Where *else* would you put a toothbrush?

DEX. (*Stops, faces her*) Giddy, this is *not* a seminar on *good housekeeping!* (*Starts for CHARLENE again*) Is *he* the reason you kept me locked out in the hall?!

CHARLENE. Of course not! Trust me!

GIDDY. We were furniture-arranging! Honest!

DEX. Don't hand me that, you two! *I* helped you move *in* here, *remember?* And every last *stick* of that bedroom furniture is right where it *always* was! How do you explain *that?*

CHARLENE. (*Is out of invention, so:*) *Tell* him, Giddy!

GIDDY. (*Inspired:*) After you went shopping I moved it all *back!*

DEX. Impossible! Even *I* can't move that *dresser* of yours without help!

GIDDY. (*As BRET re-enters from bedroom, moving down toward group*) The *plumber* gave me a hand!

DEX. He couldn't have! Plumbers have *unions! Movers* have unions! It'd be the same as crossing a *picket* line!

CHARLENE. (*Improvising fast*) Not if it's his *own* furniture!

GIDDY. (*Catching the ball*) In his own *home*!

DEX. (*Wide-eyed with surprise, to just-arriving BRET:*) And *is* it?

BRET. (*Shrugs*) Search me! I don't even recognize the toothbrush!

GIDDY. Antonio! You *can't* be through brushing *already*?

BRET. I'm *not*. I can't break the *cellophane* on the little *box*! Got something sharp?

DEX. You *live* here, and you've never unwrapped your *toothbrush*?

BRET. (*Inadvertently turns nose-to-nose with DEX again on:*) What?

DEX. (*Lurching away as before*) Never mind! I know the answer!

GIDDY. (*Urging BRET toward bedroom again*) Use the nail file in the medicine cabinet.

BRET. (*Brightens*) Good idea! Excuse me again! (*Exits to bedroom again, as DEX recovers again and:*)

DEX. (*Flailing finger bedroomward, to CHARLENE:*) *Why* is that man in his *shorts*?

GIDDY. He can *hardly* take them *off*, we have *company*!

DEX. You mean if I *wasn't* here he *would*?!

CHARLENE. What does it matter? After all, I'm a *nurse*! (*When DEX goes speechless, she tugs him kitchenward*) Now, come on, Dex, help me fix dinner, and then we can go out to a *movie*, maybe—

DEX. On Patriot's Day? Bucking those *crowds*? I thought we'd just stay *here* and watch TV!

GIDDY. With the *plumber*?

CHARLENE. *He* won't take up much room, Dex ...

DEX. Won't he be *gone* by then?

GIDDY. I doubt it. He's having dinner *with* us.

DEX. The *plumber's* joining us for *dinner?* (*Almost out of his mind*) What for?!

CHARLENE. (*Smiles weakly and shrugs, on:*) Patriot's Day!

DEX. Now, *wait* a minute—!

GIDDY. (*To "set the mood," sings:*) "Oh, beautiful for spacious skies—" (*CHARLENE sighs, and then:*)

GIDDY/CHARLENE. "—for amber waves of grain—!"

BRET. (*Re-enters from bedroom, stops just above sofa*) What *is* this, a *singalong?*

GIDDY. (*Any port in a storm*) Yes! Would you care to *join* us—?

BRET. (*Begging off with mild humor*) *You* haven't heard me *sing!*

DEX. And she's not *going* to!

GIDDY. Party-pooper!

DEX. *Whaaaat*—?!

CHARLENE. Look, if you people *want* any dinner, I'd better get out in the kitchen and—

DEX. Don't move!

GIDDY. Then how can she fix *dinner?*

DEX. Damn it, I want some *answers!*

GIDDY. But Dex, you haven't asked any *questions!*

DEX. Well, I am *going* to!

BRET. (*Conversationally, moving down from above sofa into their area*) Actually, *I* have a few questions *myself*—

DEX. (*Explodes*) *You wait your turn!*

CHARLENE. Well, maybe *he* can wait, but my *stomach* can't! Excuse me! (*Heads for kitchen again*)

DEX. But what about my *questions?*

CHARLENE. Ask *Giddy!* (*As CHARLENE exits to kitchen, fast, with groceries, BRET and DEX, eyeing one another warily, converge upon GIDDY, and:*)

DEX. Now, let's get this thing straightened out: *Why* is this man in his underwear?!

GIDDY. Why *not?* He *lives* here!

BRET. (*To DEX, hastily*) Now, look, I suppose you're wondering why I'm living with your fiancée—(*Indicates GIDDY.*)

DEX. *She's* not my fiancée! (*Points kitchenward*) *Charlene* is!

BRET. (*Turns to GIDDY, his smile not displeased*) You're *not* his fiancée? Then who *are* you?

GIDDY. Your *wife!*

DEX. (*At sea*) He didn't *know* *t*hat?

GIDDY. He's been sick.

BRET. But—I don't even know your *name!*

GIDDY. Gideon Hollis. But my friends call me "Giddy"—especially my husband!

DEX. (*Thunderstruck by developments*) Giddy—you mean you're *Mrs.* Hollis?!

GIDDY. (*Pat-a-cakes hands*) Surprise-surprise!

BRET. (*Truly baffled, to GIDDY:*) But "Hollis" isn't *Italian?!*

GIDDY. (*Embraces him rapturously, as before*) I can *dream*, can't I?

DEX. But Giddy—you *can't* be married to this guy!

GIDDY. And why *not*, may I ask?

DEX. Well, for *one* thing, you've *joined* me and Charlene on *double-dates!*

GIDDY. (*Dis-embracing BRET and confronting DEX, annoyed*) Only for *fun*. A woman gets *lonely*. And Antonio is *so* understanding!

BRET. Hold it—you said "for *one* thing," —uh—? *Who* are you, again? This isn't my day for *names*.

DEX. (*Remembers his manners*) Dex. Dexter Clayton. (*Shakes BRET's hand*) Happy to meet you.

BRET. Uh, yeah, sure, but—what was the *other* thing?

GIDDY. (*Getting worried, drags BRET back to her side, on:*) Now, darling, is this any way to celebrate our anniversary?

DEX/BRET. "Anniversary"?!

GIDDY. (*Dreamily*) Just *one* year ago today!

DEX. It *can't* be! I've been *dating* Charlene for a year!

GIDDY. So what? He's not married to *her*!

BRET. Wait, we're getting off the track. I *still* want to know what's the *other* thing Dex was going to say that makes him think we're *not* married!

DEX. I just *did* say it! I've been dating Charlene for a *year*!

GIDDY. So what does *that* prove?

DEX. If you're *married* to this guy, why haven't I ever *seen* him?

BRET. (*Turns to GIDDY*) Yeah, why?

GIDDY. (*Without hesitation*) A plumber's work is never done! (*Embraces BRET, says to DEX:*) He's hardly *ever* home!

CHARLENE. (*Enters from kitchen, carrying a martini, devoid of grocery bags*) Did I miss anything?

DEX. No, but you're just in time: Why didn't you *tell* me Giddy and Antonio were married?

CHARLENE. (*Shrugs*) You never *asked* me! (*Takes sip of drink*)

DEX. How *could* I? I didn't know there *was* an Antonio!

CHARLENE. Well, *now* you *know*. (*Takes another sip*)

BRET. (*Pulls free of GIDDY, starts backing upstage toward foyer*) Well, *I* don't! You people *say* I'm a plumber—you *say* my name's Antonio—Giddy keeps *saying* I'm *Italian*—

GIDDY. So *what*?

BRET. (*Now at brink of foyer*) So I need a *lot* more proof than *that*!

JUD. (*Appears at still-open hall door, hands behind back*) Well, *hi* there, Mister Hollis! I'm so happy to see you're up and around again! (*Brings out champagne-bottle with red-ribbon-bow around its neck*) Happy anniversary!

BRET. (*Takes proffered bottle, stares at it, then looks dazedly at GIDDY on:*) Maybe I've been *hasty...*? (*And as DEX shakes his head in puzzlement, JUD beams contentedly, and CHARLENE first rolls her eyes heavenward, then closes them and drains her drink to the bottom, and a deliriously happy GIDDY rushes into BRET's somewhat perfunctory embrace and plants a gorgeous kiss upon his not-too-displeased lips—*)

THE CURTAIN FALLS

End of Act I

ACT II

AT RISE: It is no more than two seconds later, at most. GIDDY and BRET are just wrapping up that kiss, JUD is still smiling pleasantly, and CHARLENE is just lowering emptied martini glass, which she hands to DEX, on:

CHARLENE. Hit me again.

DEX. (*Takes glass, bemused, starts for kitchen*) You want *another* martini?

CHARLENE. Try and stop me. (*DEX shrugs and exits to kitchen as GIDDY and BRET break clinch*) Finally! I was about to check your lips for *glue*!

JUD. If there's one thing I'm a sucker for, it's young people in love!

GIDDY. But Officer—it's nowhere *near* nine o'clock yet!

JUD. I'm still on duty. (*Smiles, points at champagne bottle BRET still holds*) That was a kind of afterthought, long as I had to come back here *anyhow.*

CHARLENE. (*Doesn't like the sound of this, moves U toward him*) *Had* to, Officer? I—don't understand ...

JUD. Sam *saw* me coming back to the patrol car—

CHARLENE. Sam?

GIDDY. His partner.

JUD. —so now I *have* to file my report!

GIDDY. Well, *that's* okay, Officer. Go ahead.

JUD. Trouble is, earlier, I forgot to get your husband's *first* name!

BRET. "Antonio," Officer.

45

JUD. (*Grabbing out pencil and pad; will take down pertinent facts*) Italian?

CHARLENE./BRET. (*Overlapping*) Yes!/No!

GIDDY. He's *half*-Italian. On his *mother's* side!

JUD. Ah! (*Writes it down, as DEX comes from kitchen with fresh martini*)

CHARLENE. That's why she named him "Antonio"! (*When JUD looks questioningly at her:*) She'd *hardly* call him "*Fritz*"! (*Sees DEX with drink, takes it from him on:*) Thanks! I needed that! (*Drains it to bottom; OTHERS stare at her a second; then:*)

DEX. And what would the friendly *plumber* like?

JUD. *What* plumber?

DEX. *Him!*

JUD. (*To GIDDY*) I thought you said he was a househusband?

GIDDY. He *is!* This is my house—there's my husband! Well—'bye now! (*Starts to close door in JUD's face*)

JUD. (*Presses door open; it's not hard; her move was halfhearted at best*) Wait a minute, please, I've got to get this straight for my report—is Antonio a househusband or a plumber?

BRET. (*Shrugs*) Don't ask me!

GIDDY. (*Before JUD can quite react to BRET's remark*) He's *both!* He—he *moonlights* as a plumber! We need the money desperately!

BRET. (*To GIDDY*) What *for?*

CHARLENE. (*Not smashed silly, but feeling relaxed and insouciant*) Legal fees. (*Starts for kitchen*)

DEX. You're having *another* one? (*Starts after her*)

CHARLENE. (*Muzzily, but not slurred, in tones for DEX alone, though ALL hear her:*) You can't *get* this stuff in the *pen!*

DEX. (*At sea*) You're using martini-mix to fill your *pen?*

CHARLENE. (*Giddily amused*) Of course not. The *olive* gets in the way! (*Exits to kitchen, DEX on her heels*)

JUD. (*Concerned, not suspicious*) What was all *that* about?

GIDDY. (*Desperate*) Why don't we tell you all about it at *dinner*, Officer?! (*Takes his hand with both of hers*) You haven't *had* dinner, *have* you—?

JUD. Well, *no*, but—

GIDDY. Don't you *get* a dinner-break? I mean, *before* nine o'clock?

JUD. (*Starting to warm to the idea*) Why—*yes*, I *do*! Right about *now*, as a matter of fact. But I don't want to put you folks to any trouble...?

GIDDY. It's no trouble at *all*, Officer—or may I call you "Jud"—?

JUD. (*Very pleased*) Why, *sure*, Mrs. Hollis—I mean, if I'm gonna be *eating* with you—!

CHARLENE. (*Just re-entering from kitchen with fresh martini*) You *are*?!

BRET. (*A bit muddled by everything, but amiable*) She just invited him.

GIDDY. (*To JUD*) And you can call me "Giddy"!

CHARLENE. (*This time* unheard *by OTHERS*) With good reason! (*Takes sip of drink as DEX emerges from kitchen behind her*)

JUD. Oh, but I'd better tell Sam. Be back in a minute, folks! (*Exits down hall, GIDDY swiftly shutting door after him, even during:*)

CHARLENE. (*Sociably, but also sincerely*) Take your time! (*To herself*) Maybe we can get through dessert before the SWAT team arrives! (*Sips her drink*)

DEX. What—?

CHARLENE. Nothing. It's just the *olive* talking.

DEX. Honey, are you sure you're in *shape* to fix dinner?

CHARLENE. (*This sobers her*) Dinner! I haven't even *started* it! What was I *thinking* of?! (*To GIDDY*) Don't *answer* that! (*Drains drink*) Excuse me! (*Exits to kitchen*)

BRET. (*Moving down into room, GIDDY trailing him*) Does she *always* drink like that?

DEX. You tell *me*! You *live* with her! Say! I just *thought* of something!

CHARLENE. (*Appears as if propelled by a spring, popping in from kitchen so fast that she has to grab doorjamb to stop herself in room; she looks* very *sober now, and not terribly happy*) What?

GIDDY. (*Helpfully*) Dex just thought of something.

CHARLENE. I don't mean what-I-didn't-*hear*-you, I mean what-did-he-just-*think*-of!

DEX. There's only *one bed* in your bedroom!

BRET. (*Can see dismay on CHARLENE's face, misinterprets*) A *gentleman* wouldn't *know* about Charlene's bedroom!

DEX. (*Means How He Knows*) I have to use the *bathroom*—?!

GIDDY. *Again*?

DEX. I mean *every-so-often*, damn it! And I *see* the bed as I walk *by!*

CHARLENE. (*Praying that confusion will shift the subject*) You mean *run* by, don't you?!

GIDDY. (*Catches her ploy, joins it:*) You really ought to have a *checkup*, Dex!

DEX. (*Having none of it*) Whoa! We're getting off the subject!

BRET. *What* subject?

DEX. That *bedroom*, with only *one bed!*

GIDDY. But it's a *king-size*. We have *plenty* of room!

DEX. (*Starting to glower toward BRET.*) For *how many* ?

CHARLENE. *Two*, darling!

GIDDY. One of us sleeps on the *sofa!*

DEX. *Which* one?!

CHARLENE. *Antonio*, of course!

GIDDY. That's why I had Jud *put* him there!

BRET. On the *sofa*? Then why did I wake up in the *bedroom*?

GIDDY. It was a *special treat!* You were all worn out from the *race!*

DEX. Hold it—*hold it*—HOLD IT! (*They hold it*) If you two have been *married* all year, why don't you sleep *together*?

BRET. (*Puzzled, to GIDDY*) Hey, yeah, why *don't* we?

CHARLENE. (*Without thinking it through*) Antonio snores!

DEX. How do *you* know?

CHARLENE. *Giddy* told me!

GIDDY. How *else* would she find out?

DEX. (*Not quite purple, but close*) That's what *I'm* trying to find out! (*To BRET*) Just what goes *on* in this apartment nights?

GIDDY. We sleep, he snores.

CHARLENE. Now that *that's* settled, how about getting that champagne on *ice*, huh?!

BRET. (*Almost forgot he was holding bottle*) Oh! Oh, yeah, sure thing! (*Starts for kitchen*) Where's the ice-bucket?

DEX. (*Exits after him, very suspicious*) You don't *know*?!

GIDDY. (*Calls after him*) It's *brand-new*, Dex! I forgot to tell him where I put it! (Sotto voce *to CHARLENE.*) Where *did* I put it?

BRET. (*Off*) Which cabinet, Giddy?

CHARLENE. (Sotto voce *to GIDDY [look, let's save lots of ink and stage-directions: people who go into* huddles *in this play* naturally *lower their voices]*) We don't *have* an ice-bucket!

GIDDY. How quick can we *get* one?

CHARLENE. Tomorrow morning when the stores open!

GIDDY. Won't that be too late?

DEX. (*Off*) *Charlene—?*

CHARLENE. It's *already* too late! (*Then louder, toward DEX:*) I forgot! It's broken! Leaks like crazy, all over the place!

GIDDY. Just put the bottle and some ice in the *sink*, Antonio!

BRET. (*Off*) Okay, honey!

DEX. (*Off*) I hope you saved the receipt!

CHARLENE. *What* receipt?

GIDDY. (*To CHARLENE*) It's *new*, remember? We just *bought* it!

DEX. (*Off*) *What* did she say—?

CHARLENE. It'll keep! (*Tows GIDDY farther D, her manner growing increasingly frantic*) This won't work. Nothing will work. They're mad at each other, and that cop's coming back, and— (*Realizes*) Hey! Why in blazes *did* you invite the *fuzz* to join us at dinner?!

GIDDY. (*Brightly*) To avert *suspicion*, of course! He was starting to give me a *funny look.*

CHARLENE. (*Wearily*) By the time he gets through chatting some more with *Antonio*, the look he's giving you will be positively *hilarious!*

GIDDY. We just won't *sit* him next to Antonio.

CHARLENE. Giddy, we won't be at the *table!* Our little kitchenette booth can squeeze in *four* people—and *that's* a very tight *maybe!* We'll have to serve dinner *buffet-*style and eat out *here!*

GIDDY. Don't worry. We'll manage. Somehow.

CHARLENE. No we won't. And do you know why? Because it's hard enough *walking* on eggs, Gideon Hollis—and *you* keep *dancing* on them!

DEX. (*Entering with two glasses of champagne from kitchen*) Dancing? We barely have room to *walk* in this place!

CHARLENE. Dex! You came back!

DEX. I was *only* in the *kitchen*, honey! Here, have some champagne! (*To GIDDY, as he hands CHARLENE one of the glasses*) Antonio's bringing yours.

BRET. (*Entering from kitchen with two more champagne glasses*) And here it is! Happy anniversary!

GIDDY. (*Takes glass from him*) Darling! You remembered! How nice!

CHARLENE. (*Dully, thoughts of ultimate doom flitting across her face*) Yes, isn't it!

GIDDY. (*Takes small sip*) Mmmm, that's good! How'd you get it so cold so fast?

BRET. Apparently that policeman—

GIDDY. Jud Keegan.

BRET. Apparently Jud *bought* it chilled!

CHARLENE. Why didn't I hear the *cork* pop?

DEX. (*With a semi-sigh*) It was a screw-top bottle.

GIDDY. Oh, well. It's the *thought* that counts!

CHARLENE. Right!

DEX. I think a toast is in order: To Gideon and Antonio: The cutest couple in Boston's Back Bay!

BRET. (*Blinks*) *Where* did you say?

DEX. "Back Bay," of course. Where did you *think* we were? I mean, you were running in the *marathon*—you *must* know where it *ends*...?

BRET. *I* was in the *marathon*?! (*A bit confused, obviously starting to almost remember things*) Wait—*that's* what you meant—a moment ago—you said I was worn out from the *race*—so sleeping in the bedroom was a *special treat*—! But—I thought—I thought you meant—worn out from *watching* the race, not *running* in it!

GIDDY. Why, of *course* you were running in it! Running so hard that you wore all the traction off your track shoes! (*To CHARLENE.*) The bottoms were smooth as glass!

DEX. (*For the first time looks closely at BRET's feet*) Hey, those are *dress* shoes!

CHARLENE. (*Doesn't like where this is going, strives to cover all bases*) No *wonder* he lost the race!

DEX. Wait a minute—if Antonio *wasn't* entered in the race—then these aren't *running-* shorts he's wearing!

GIDDY. (*Looks downward at BRET, realizes, screams:*) Antonio! You're in your *undershorts*! (*Now both women scream, and turn their backs, avoiding looking at him*)

BRET. (*Logically*) Even if I *am*—what's the problem? They don't *look* any different from before—?!

DEX. (*Man-to-man*) It's just a woman-thing, Antonio. Women react to clothing by its *name*, not its appearance!

BRET. (*Nods*) You mean like when they scream if you see them in a *bra*, but not when you see even *more* of them in a *bikini*? (*Nods*) Exactly! (*BOTH men take a sip of champagne, rather suavely; then:*)

CHARLENE. (*Still facing upstage, as is GIDDY*) Antonio, if you *don't* mind, would you kindly put something *on*?!

GIDDY. (*Realizes, turns her head to face CHARLENE.—but not far enough to embarrass BRET*) Such as—?!

CHARLENE. (*Also realizes, if a little late*) Oh! Oh, that's right!

DEX. What's right?

CHARLENE. He—he *can't* put something on—because—because—

BRET. Because why?

CHARLENE. *You* tell him Giddy!

GIDDY. (*Thinks a second; then:*) All your clothes are at the cleaners!

DEX./BRET. *All* of them?!

GIDDY. (*Shrugs*) You almost *never* go out on Patriot's Day! It seemed like a good time.

BRET. To do what? Run around in my underwear?

GIDDY. To take all your clothes to the cleaners!

DEX. I can't believe it! A Bostonian who doesn't go out to watch the *marathon*?

GIDDY. He watches on TV!

CHARLENE. Hates crowds!

BRET. (*Sets emptied champagne glass on desk, fingers go to temples*) No ... no, wait ... that's not right ... I *enjoy* the crowds ... the excitement ... I *always* go to Copley Square to watch the *finish*—!

DEX. Dressed like *that*?!

GIDDY. (*BOTH women now turn once again to face MEN, ignoring BRET's undress*) But you *must* have been in the race! What else would make you *collapse*?

BRET. (*A part of his memory returns; he declaims, as astounded as his audience:*) I was *mugged*! It's coming back! They took all my clothes—my wallet—

DEX. This is monstrous! What did they *do* — sandbag you?

BRET. (*Trying desperately to recall*) No ... I was in the crowd—everybody packed up close—these *men* were *especially* close to me—then all at once, one of them put something over my *face*, and—!

CHARLENE. *Chloroform*! Of course! *That's* the rotten smell on his breath! (*Smacks palm to her forehead*) How *could* I forget his lousy *smell*?!

BRET. (*Insulted*) I *beg* your pardon!

GIDDY. Not *now*, Antonio, she means before you brushed your *teeth*!

BRET. (*Mollified*) Oh. Oh, yeah, right. Now I remember. I couldn't stand the smell *myself*! (*To DEX*) That's why I brushed.

DEX. And don't think I'm not grateful. (*Suddenly realizes*) Say, that *cop* who's coming back here better *not* go off duty! We have a *crime* to report! (*Sets glass on desk, starts toward hall door*) Maybe I can catch him before his partner drives off to dinner—

CHARLENE. (*Terrified by now, rushes after him*) Wait! It's too late! Those muggers are *long* gone, Dex—!

DEX. (*Stops, turns, for:*) Charlene, I love you dearly, but this is a matter of *civic duty*! (*Turns and will exit to hall, CHARLENE scrambling after him on:*)

CHARLENE. But you *can't*! They'll want you to go downtown and sign a *statement* and we haven't had our *dinner* yet—(*They are gone*)

BRET. Yipe! I hope *I* don't have to go downtown—dressed like *this*!

GIDDY. (*Brightens*) You *don't*! I have *just* the thing for you to wear! (*Starts for bedroom*) It's stored in a bottom drawer, but I'm *sure* it'll fit you!

BRET. *What* will fit me?

GIDDY. (*Stops just short of exit*) A pants-suit. It was my mother's. Many years ago.

BRET. (*Softly sympathetic*) She died...?

GIDDY. She couldn't *stand* it. (*Exits to bedroom, her voice trailing away on:*) If I snip off some of the *sequins*, I'm *sure* no one will look at you funny—!

BRET. (*Appalled at this image*) But *Giddy*—!

GIDDY. (*Off*) *I* don't mind the work, darling! Won't be more than a few minutes!

BRET. (*Means if he goes downtown like that*) But what am I going to *do* if—?

GIDDY. (*Off*) I *said* I won't be *long*, Antonio! Why don't you watch *TV* while I *masculinize* it a little?

BRET. (*Gives up, shrugs*) May as well! (*He will now go to TV, switch it on, and then move to armchair to sit and watch it [NOTE: The screen* needn't *be seen by the theatre audience, but if you* have *a VCR, and a talented "anchorman"-type for this point in the show, by* all *means go visual], getting already seated before the message on the TV starts to* register *on him*)

ANCHORMAN. (*On TV*) ... far into the night, as always, with flags, pennants, music and dance. Even the losers have fun at the Patriot's Day festivities! (*Shifts vocal gears to somber*) On the *serious* side of the news: The two men arrested today as suspects in the disappearance of financier-millionaire Bret Fleming (*BRET reacts, sits bolt upright, fingers to temples*) continue to disavow any knowledge of his whereabouts. Captured late this afternoon when one of them attempted to make a purchase with the missing man's credit card, (*BRET is slowly coming to his feet, his eyes glued to the screen*) the men insist they left their victim unconscious-but-unharmed in Copley Square, making their getaway through the heavy crowds observing the finish of today's race. No sign of the missing millionaire—shown here in a recent snapshot—(*BRET rushes to the screen for a closer look, his fingertips going to his face, recognition and memory coming to life*) has yet been found. Any persons with information leading to the locating of the victim should contact their local police department and—(*BRET snaps off TV, straightens up slowly, looks up in direction of bedroom, from which we can now hear GIDDY HUMMING happily [something very Italian would be appropriate here— "Come Back to Sorrento," "Santa Lucia," or some such, not with words, but more of a "da-dee-dum-dee-dah-dee" approach] as she de-sequins that pants-suit; his face clouds with fury, and he turns and strides purposefully toward telephone; then, just as he puts his hand upon phone, he pauses and looks bedroomward again; the clouds slowly scatter from his face, replaced with a kind of tender smile; he looks down at his state-of-undress, shakes his head, then suppresses a near-laugh; GIDDY's humming will peter out slowly, now, as she perhaps increases her concentration on her task, and as BRET—with his head turned bedroomward—slowly lowers himself onto deskchair; then, furtively, looking almost guilty, he lifts receiver and dials a number on the phone; while he waits for his party, he spots that bottle of wine DEX had arrived with, turns it with his free hand, then picks it up so he can read the label; he scowls in distaste, sets bottle back upon desk, and deliberately turns label toward wall; then:)*

BRET. *(Gets his party, leans foward in a kind of seated crouch, speaks with voice lowered, hastily and urgently:)* Jacobsen? ... It's Mister Fleming! ... Yes-yes, I'm fine, just fine! ... I don't have *time* to explain now, I'll fill you in later ... No, you can have them call off the search ... No, *that* part's true, I *was* mugged, but I'm okay now ... *(Suddenly stern)* Of *course* I want them prosecuted! ... You bet I do! ... But can you go down to the station and get my wallet and credit-cards back? ... Clothes—? *(Looks bedroomward, smiles, shakes his head, turns back to phone)* No, just have them cleaned—or if they're too beat up, throw 'em away. I've already made *other* arrangements for clothing—*(Casts uncertain glance bedroomward, adds:)*—I hope! ... But I need you to get *over* here with my wallet ... Because—well—I think I have a *date* tonight! ... No-no, it is a long story ... *Where?* I haven't the foggiest notion. Why don't I leave the phone off the hook when we've finished and you can have the number traced? ... Good, good ... *No*, don't come with the *police*! Everything's just fine! ... *(Glance bedroomward; then, on phone again, rapturously:)* Couldn't be finer ... That's right. Just my wallet. Great ... Okay, see you then!

(*Almost sets phone down, but suddenly lifts it to his face again for:*) Wait. One more thing.—Uh—Jacobsen, I *know* this is going to sound kind of silly, and hardly the sort of thing a boss asks his personal secretary, but—well—just between you and me—man to man—would you answer one small question? ... (*Very surreptitious look bedroomward, then leans into even tighter sit-crouch, and, on phone, asks wistfully, hopefully, plaintively:*) Do *I* look *Italian*—?! ... (*The reply obviously pleases him; he sits up straight, beaming, and we know what the reply must have been as he completes his conversation:*) Grazie! [GROT-zee-ay] (*BRET stands, looks at receiver, makes a decision, slides open center drawer of desk and starts to place receiver inside it with care, then abruptly thinks of something, whips receiver out again and to his face:*) Jacobsen—? Oh, good, you're still there! Just one more thing—I want you to make dinner reservations—for *two*—at my favorite restaurant for—oh—about an hour from now ... Yes, yes, I *know* what Patriot's Day is like, but *surely*— ... Yeah, I guess that's one of the *perks* of being a millionaire, all right! ... Say, I just got a *better* idea! Never mind the phone-trace. Just *meet* me with my wallet, at the restaurant! ... Right! ... Great ... See you there! (*Hangs up phone, shuts desk drawer, then moves carefully up to area just D of foyer, looking bedroomward, a strange smile on his face; he stops there, rubs his hands together briefly in glee, says* sotto voce:) This is going to be *fun*—! (*Then calls out, in normal tones:*) Giddy, honey, how's it going?

GIDDY. (*Off*) Slowly-but-surely, Antonio! Takes awhile, because Mother was such a *big* woman, you know, and there's *lots* of sequins! But I'm getting 'em, I'm getting 'em! (*Sudden pause, then, with surprised realization:*) Antonio! You—you called me "*honey*"—!

BRET. (*Enjoying every minute of his ploy*) What's wrong with *that*? After all—you're my *wife* ... right?

GIDDY. (*Off; pause; then:*) Oh, absolutely! Yessiree!

BRET. I can hardly wait to see my anniversary present!

GIDDY. (*Off; pause; then:*) Your *what*?!

BRET. Anniversary present. It's our anniversary. On anniversaries, people give presents.

GIDDY. (*Off*) Oh, but *we* don't!

BRET. We don't? Why not?

GIDDY. (*Off*) It—it was *your* idea, sweetheart, remember—?

BRET. (*Shakes his head, amused, in a gotta-hand-it-to-this-gal appreciation of her quick-on-the-uptake improvisations; then:*) What gave me a silly idea like *that*—?

GIDDY. (*Off; has had time to think, now, so answers at once:*) All the *other* presents!

BRET. *What* other presents?

GIDDY. (*Off*) Oh, you know: First-*week* anniversary, then first-*month* anniversary, and so on and so on. You've always been such a *romantic!* But frankly, we can't *afford* it!

BRET. We could afford the *other* presents...!?

GIDDY. (*Off*) *No* we couldn't. Not *really*, I mean. The plumbing business has been in a real slump, lately, and with that puny little salary I make at the *museum*—!

BRET. Museum?

GIDDY. (*Off; long pause; then:*) Oh, honey, I guess I forgot to tell you: I've got a job! I'm assistant curator at the Museum of Fine Arts!

BRET. How wonderful! We can *use* the extra income. When did you *get* it?

GIDDY. (*Off; without thinking*) Three years ago! ... (*With horror:*) That is—I mean—?!

BRET. (*Can hardly keep from laughing aloud, controls his voice on:*) You had the job when we got married? Why didn't you *tell* me?

GIDDY (*Off; not enjoying the conversation at all, almost frantic*) You were always so *busy*. Out *plumbing*.

BRET. I thought business was in a slump?

GIDDY (*Off*) Not *all* the time!

BRET. Honey, you're not making sense!

GIDDY. (*Off; in almost a sob*) I never do!

BRET. I mean, *why* didn't you tell me during one of my *slumps*?

GIDDY. (*Off; has The Answer; responds brightly:*) Because *I* was out working. You were home slumping.

BRET. (*Out front, with* sotto voce *admiration*) Wow. She ... is ... good! (*Then, back toward bedroom:*) Hey, how much longer? I'm getting kind of chilly out here. (*Starts R*) Maybe I should come in there ...

GIDDY. (*Off; panicky*) Where? You mean in here?! But this is the bedroom!

BRET. (*Stops just short of exit*) So what? What *better* place for a man and wife on their anniversary?

GIDDY. (*Off*) *Not* while I'm removing *sequins*!

BRET. Why *not*?

GIDDY. (*Off; improvising frantically*) Because ... because ... it's *bad luck* for a man to watch his wife removing sequins—especially on their anniversary!

BRET. Where did you get a silly notion like *that*?

GIDDY. (*Off; slowly, because another part of her mind is* composing) It's ... it's an old maxim ... from a sampler my grandmother was stitching ... when I was a little girl ...

BRET. *What* maxim?

GIDDY. (*Off; has had enough time, now; recites carefully:*) The bride who lets a sequin drop ... Will find her marriage at Full Stop ... If seen by her groom on their anniversary ...

BRET. (*Can see she's stymied, but smilingly insists:*) Go *on*, darling...?

GIDDY. (*Off; hopelessly glum and gloomy, knowing this is just terrible:*) And lovelife goes from *bad* to *worsery*!

BRET. That's quite a sampler!

GIDDY. (*Off; we can* hear *the shrug in her voice:*) She was quite a grandmother! Now will you *stop* this constant *interrupting* or I'll *never* get this done before *dinner*!

BRET. I don't absolutely *need* the suit to have dinner ...

GIDDY. (*Off*) What if you spill *coffee* in your lap? You want it on bare skin or absorbent velvet?

BRET. (*Slightly shaken*) "*Velvet*"? Giddy—this pants-suit you're fixing—

GIDDY. (*Off*) *Lots* of men wear velvet pants!

BRET. But Giddy—!

GIDDY. (*Off*) Stop *worrying* about it! Mother had *wonderful* taste in *clothes*!

BRET. But those are *women's* clothes!

GIDDY. (*Off*) Not so's you'd *notice* it—Mother was on the *large* side—a regular *Amazon*—!

BRET. (*As-if-casually*) You mean one of those gals who used to raid the villages and carry men off for *mating* purposes...?

GIDDY. (*Off; after a* long *pause*) Uh. Yes. I guess you *could* say that ... Why—why do you *ask* ... darling?

BRET. Just wondered if *you* maybe could have inherited some of her traits, that's all.

GIDDY. (*Off; laughs giddily, but with an edge of panic; then:*) Don't be silly! Mother never carried *anyone* off— unless you count *Father*. (*Quickly adds:*) Don't get me *wrong*—he wasn't exactly a *runt*—but he *did* have this bad back—and since Mother was so big and strong anyway ... (*An abrupt near-growl*) Oh, never mind! (*Without warning, GIDDY emerges from bedroom, carrying a garment, and hands it to him [it is velvet, and a rather wild cerise in color]*) Here are the pants! The coat'll be ready in a minute!

(*Turns to re-enter bedroom, but BRET tosses pants over back of sofa, grabs her by the shoulders, spins her around, pulls her into his arms, growling huskily:*)

BRET. What's your hurry ... darling?

GIDDY. (*Terrified*) No hurry! No hurry at all! Happy anniversary! Now let me go!

BRET. (*Embracing her more thoroughly*) Aw, c'mon, sweetheart! This is our golden opportunity!

GIDDY. Opportunity for *what?*

BRET. Charlene's gone ... Dexter is gone ... we have the place to ourselves ... and it's been *so* lonely sleeping on that *sofa...*

GIDDY. (*Stares up into his face a moment, breathing rather hard, mostly from terror, but with just a hint of passions, too; then, As If She Didn't Know The Answer, in a timid, teeny-tiny-mouse voice, squeaks:*) What did you have in mind?

BRET. (*Will continually try to connect his lips with hers, over:*) Oh, darling!

GIDDY. (*Will continually evade those lips of his, over:*) Now, Antonio—

BRET. My little lover-lump!

GIDDY. Please—

BRET. (*Inspired, starts going Italian:*) *Cara mia!* [KAH-rah *mee*-ah]

GIDDY. Oh, don't! Please don't! Not *that!*

BRET. *Mi amore!* [mee ah-MOH-ray]

GIDDY. Stop! Stop, I'm getting all *melty* inside!

BRET. *Mi bella bambina!* [mee BAYL-lah bahm-*bee*-nah]

GIDDY. *My,* but it's getting hot in here! (*Manages to squirm free enough to slide the curtains apart*) I've got to open a *window*—!

BRET. (*Clasps her closer, the two of them* writhing *before the window*) No. No air. No nothing. Nothing but you ... and me ... and this magical night!

GIDDY. No, wait, please, stop, you're getting me all *sweaty!* (*Twists free, rushes around sofa and down toward kitchen*)

BRET. (*Turns, is about to follow, remembers, looks to his left out window, gives a cheery wave to the "binocular brigade," on:*) Ladies, this is your lucky night! (*Then hurries down after GIDDY, on:*) Come, my little gondola of love, we shall make big waves together!

GIDDY. But *I* can't *swiiiiim...!* (*This is a shriek of mortal terror and she flees into the kitchen with BRET in hot pursuit, and then we hear:*) Stand *back!* I've got a *banana!* ... *Two* bananas! ... *Three* bananas! Damn it, Antonio, can't you take a hint?!

BRET. (*Off; in quasi-Italian accent*) Of-a course-a! You gotta the three banan'! It means-a you wanna *monkey around!*

GIDDY. Noooooo .....! (*Her long-lasting wail starts "off" but continues as she rushes on, in a headlong hurtling lurch that ends with her diving over L end of sofa and landing face down there, but rolling U onto her back as BRET does near-identical entrance and yet, even while he is in mid-air over sofa, she manages to* reverse-roll *and plop onto floor in front of sofa as he sprawls face down on the cushions; struggling to get up, she shouts:*) Wait! Stop! You've got it all wrong! Let me explain! You don't understand!

BRET. (*Swings his feet to the floor, stands [facing R], grabs her hands and pulls her to her feet facing him; then, in a no-nonsense voice:*) All right. Explain. (*They're barely a handsbreadth apart; GIDDY looks up at him, her face crumples, and suddenly she's weeping into her hands;*

BRET caves in) Aw, don't do that—I hate it when women do *that—stop* it!

GIDDY. (*Uncovers her face*) I c-c-can't! (*Recovers face, sobs again*)

BRET. (*Trying to be stern, but very irresolute*) Oh ... oh ... ohhhhh—! (*Grabs the sides of her shoulders*) Here— (*Will seat her gently onto sofa, his own motions mirroring hers a fraction of a second later, till both are seated on D lip of sofa cushion, bodies at arm's-length apart, but inner knees touching, during:*) Just—sit. Sit down here—relax. And *please* stop that sobbing, I can't stand it!

GIDDY. (*Hands still on face, splays her fingers enough to peek at him*) You can't?

BRET. I should be *gloating* at your unhappiness, considering what you've done, but— no. I can't do it. Here— (*Neither of them realizing how silly it looks, he lifts near cuff of those velvet pants hanging over back of sofa between them and dabs at her eyes with it a moment; she helps with the dabbing; then:*) Better...?

GIDDY. (*Nods, her voice just short of the brink of tears*) Uh-huh. Thank you, Antonio—

BRET. (*A tinge of return to stern, warningly:*) Giddy—!

GIDDY. (*Amends*)—or *whoever* you are, I mean.

BRET. (*This aspect hadn't occurred to him*) You don't *know* who I am?

GIDDY. (*Blankly*) No. *Should* I? Who *are* you?

BRET. (*Almost tells her; hesitates; then:*) Let's—just let that go for a moment, shall we?

GIDDY. (*A piteous little shrug*) If you say so.

BRET. Good. Now—why don't you *tell* me about it— all of it.

GIDDY. (*With fair control, her voice trembling but not breaking*) See ... all my life ... I've been *looking* for an Antonio ... or at least his *type* ...

BRET. I don't follow that—?

GIDDY. The *Italian* type—at least, *my* idea of it—big—hearty—warm—handsome—friendly—

BRET. (*Sympathetically*) I think I get the idea. Go on.

GIDDY. And you—well—when I first set eyes on you today—

BRET. *First*? This is the first time you've ever *seen* me—or at least a *picture* of me—?

GIDDY. I don't understand. Where would I see a picture of you? Are you saying we went to school together, or something, and I'd recognize you from the yearbook—?

BRET. Uh—well—*something* like that, yes.

GIDDY. (*Less weepy, a little joyous*) Really? Which *class* were you in? Were you on the basketball team, or—?

BRET. No-no-no, I wasn't. Let's skip over that part and get back to this afternoon.

GIDDY. This afternoon?

BRET. In Copley Square.

GIDDY. Oh. That. Well—? (*Raises her shoulders in a slow shrug, fingers wide, palms upward*) It's—kind of hard to explain—

BRET. (*Gently*) Try.

GIDDY. (*Getting sort of melancholy-happy emotional as she speaks*) I was watching the race ... and the last runner had come in ... except that I thought *you* were the last runner, the way you were *dressed* ...

BRET. I know, I know. Go ahead.

GIDDY. And there was a kind of *crowd* around you—you know how people are—they like to *look* at unconscious bodies, but nobody *does* anything about them—nobody—nobody seems to care ...

BRET. (*Nods*) Ain't *that* the truth! America—the Home of Non-Involvement!

GIDDY. The what?

BRET. I was just saying what *you* just said, in different words.

GIDDY. Oh. Well—anyhow ... There you *were*—kind of flopped on your side—with a lock of hair dangling over your forehead, and—and—well— (*Abruptly takes his hands, smiling wistfully into his face*) —I just thought you were the most beautiful sight I'd ever seen in my life! And when that policeman came over—that Jud Keegan, I mean—and said, "Anybody know this guy?"—well—I found myself saying, "*I* do!" I don't know *why* I said that ... no, wait, I *do* know why! There was *something*—I can't describe it—just something about you—lying there, so pale and helpless—and—oh—I suddenly felt that—that you and I had known each other all our lives! (*Semi-tightens her clutch on his hands*) Know what I mean—? (*Almost by magnetism, their faces are slowly drawing nearer and nearer to one another's, and this will continue relentlessly during:*)

BRET. (*Huskily*) Do I ever! (*Swallows*)

GIDDY. I just couldn't *leave* you there—and I couldn't let them take you *away*—all at once, all I wanted in the whole wide world was to *be* with you when you woke up—to *tell* you what I was feeling—to see your face light up like a rainbow and hear you say that *you* felt the same way...! Crazy, wasn't I.

BRET. (*Their lips are now millimeters apart*) Not even slightly.

GIDDY. So I said you *belonged* to me—said you were my *husband*—so Jud would *bring* you here—because—because—?

BRET. (*Finishing for her*) —because once you've found the only one you'll ever love, you must never let her *go* ...

GIDDY. (*Though palpitating with anticipation, feels obliged to say:*) Never let *him* go ...

BRET. Depends on one's point of view ...

GIDDY. (*Nods longingly*) So many things *do* ...

BRET. (*Can stand it no longer, his arms reach out for her—*) Oh, Giddy—!

GIDDY. (—*As her arms reach out for him*) *Oh, Whoever*—! (*And for about ten seconds, we get to watch the most marvelous clinch in the history of the theatre; once* that's *out of the way:*)

BRET. (*Stands*) We've got to talk. Got to go somewhere and talk.

GIDDY. (*Stands*) But *where*? In *Boston* on *Patriot's Day* you can hardly find room on the *sidewalks*!

BRET. I know a very nice restaurant—

GIDDY. But—*Charlene's* making dinner—?!

BRET. For herself and Dex. Believe me, they'd prefer it that way.

GIDDY. But what about *Jud*? I mean, I *invited* him—?!

BRET. I'm sure they won't mind *one* more mouth to feed—if he doesn't stay too long.

GIDDY. Oh, Antonio—or whoever—! It sounds absolutely *dreamy*—but to *find* a place—?!

BRET. Trust me. I have a few connections. (*Swings her D-then-L so she's clear to move U*) Now get *in* there and finish de-feminizing that *coat*!

GIDDY. (*Goes to attention, gives a snappy salute*) *Si-si, mi capitan*! [see-SEE mee KAH-pee-TAHN] (*Turns and hurries toward exit to bedroom*)

BRET. Hey, go easy on the foreign languages, lady! When *we* have our little talk, I want everything in *English*!

GIDDY. (*Stops just short of exit, gives a curved-forefinger-touch just above her eyebrow, like a very casual salute, on:*) Right-ho, guv'nor! (*Bolts off to bedroom even as he shouts after her:*)

BRET. I didn't mean *British*—! (*But she is gone; chuckling, and very happy, he hastens to phone, gives one quick look back toward bedroom, then dials quickly, speaks softly:*) ... Jacobsen, it's me! ... I was afraid I wouldn't catch you! ... Listen, just a *slight* change of plan—unless you think they'll *let* me into the Ritz-Carlton Restaurant wearing a red velvet lady's pants-suit? ... Yes, that *is* what I'll be wearing! ... But that's why I called—better bring me some clothes *after* all ... The works ... I can change in the back of the limo ... Right! ... Thanks, you're a treasure! (*Hangs up phone, and just as he does so, CHARLENE, DEX and JUD enter at front door; their faces are a bit in shock, and DEX carries a folded newspaper in one hand; they stop just below foyer, uneasily*)

DEX. Uh—*Antonio* ... Have—um—?

CHARLENE. Have you seen the *papers*?

JUD. Your picture's all over the front page—! (*Abruptly removes his cap, deferentially, appends:*) —sir ...

BRET. (*This could Blow Everything; he waves them kitchenward, with a sort of hoarse-but-hushed shout:*) Quiet, you idiots! Not another word! Get in here before she hears you! (*"Here" referring to the kitchen, of course; they scurry to obey:*)

DEX. Right!

JUD. You bet!

CHARLENE. Gotcha! (*BRET follows the scurriers off, L, herding them out of sight; then:*)

GIDDY. (*Off*) Did I hear somebody come *in*—?

OTHERS (*Off*) NOOOOO—!

GIDDY. (*Off*) Okay, honey. Only be a minute more—!

NEWCOMERS (*Off; with less volume:*) "Honey"—?!

BRET. (*Off; low, conspiratorial voice*) It's a long story. Now, pay attention—! (*For about five seconds, we hear nothing but GIDDY's HUM-SINGING some Italianate melody, as before; then FOURSOME comes out of kitchen, no longer as hushed, but careful not to let their voices carry to the bedroom, either, moving on tiptoe into a kind of DC "football huddle" and speaking even as they scuttle to assemble there:*)

JUD. (*To BRET*) By rights, I ought to run you in—and the two ladies with you!

BRET. For *what*—being kidnapped without a *permit*?

JUD. You should've called the police!

BRET. If you will check your nine-one-one records for this afternoon—and I seem to recall they *tape* every syllable of every call—you will find that I *did* call the cops, loud and long!

JUD. And they didn't *come*?

BRET. If they *came*, would I still *be* here?

CHARLENE. What *I* want to know is why you don't *tell* her who you are!

BRET. Because for the first time in my life—a not-very-long but definitely very *lonely* life—I have met a lovely young girl who likes *me*! Not my money—not my fame—not my social position—me, alone, a man she found lying in his shorts in a public street! Frankly—it's wonderful!

DEX. When do you *plan* to tell her—on your silver anniversary?!

BRET. *When* I tell Giddy is none of your business! The point is, *you* are not to tell her, *none* of you!

JUD. But, darn it all, I've got to press *charges* against her, for *kidnapping* you!

BRET. *Why*? *I'm* not pressing charges, am I?

JUD. But what'll I say in my *report*?

BRET. Hell, *I* don't know! Say it was all—some kind of *mistake*!

CHARLENE. Like, maybe, you and Giddy knew each other *already*—?

DEX. And maybe you *were* really in the race, but running *incognito*—!

JUD. And *what*? She had me tote you up here so's not to *blow* your *cover*?!

CHARLENE. What's wrong with *that*?

JUD. It's the *stupidest* alibi I ever heard in my *life*, *that's* what!

DEX. So why did you come *up* with it?

BRET. Oh, let's *stop* all this silly squabbling—are you with me, or are you not?!

DEX. Well, of course, *I'm* in favor of anything that keeps *Charlene* out of the pokey!

CHARLENE. But, it'll be such a *shock* to poor Giddy when she learns she's being romanced by a *millionaire*—!

JUD. (*Sincerely*) *I* should have such a shock! The best *I* could do on the social scale was dating a famous *horsewoman!*

DEX. (*Uncertainly*) A *jockey?*

JUD. (*Glumly*) A *nag!*

GIDDY. (*Off; carols happily*) *All* done, darling! Ready or not, here I come!

BRET. (*Quickly*) Come on, everybody. What do you say? (*Extends his hand toward them, fingers together, palm downward*) Deal—?

TRIO. (*After a fractional hesitation, they pile one hand apiece atop his, in a mutual "pact"-stack, and say in I-give-up voices in unison:*) Deal. (*Then ALL straighten up and disperse variously [DEX to stand with hand atop TV, leaning idly, CHARLENE to sit C of sofa, JUD to head toward kitchen, and BRET to move up toward foyer area], on:*)

DEX. Wonder if there's any good shows tonight?

JUD. *Where* did you say you put those smoked oysters? (*Exits*)

CHARLENE. They're in the bag under the beer nuts!

BRET. (*Addressing GIDDY, who now enters, proudly holding up jacket toward him*) Wow! That's—that's certainly *red*, isn't it!

GIDDY. Try it on! Please!

BRET. (*Takes pants from sofa-back*) Better do these first—(*Is right in front of window, facing D, starts to bend forward to get into pants, remembers, flicks a glance windowward, and then sidles about two steps L, so as not to give the old ladies a treat; while he struggles into pants, and then into jacket:)*

GIDDY. (*Notices CHARLENE and DEX*) Oh! You came back!

DEX. (*Shrugs*) I was *invited.*

CHARLENE. (*Shrugs*) I *live* here!

GIDDY. (*Thrilled*) Antonio's taking me out!

BRET. (*Still struggling into clothes*) "Antonio"?

GIDDY. I *have* to call you *something*—!

BRET. Fair enough.

CHARLENE. (*Glances on either side of her, then toward desk, then armchair*) Say, what became of my magazine?

DEX. (*Moves to sofa, sits beside her, during:*) Charlene, the man you love above all others on the face of the earth is right within your grasp, and you're going to sit here and *read*—?!

CHARLENE. No, of course not, but there was this neat-o article I wanted to show you, all about the latest public misbehavior of [*NOTE: Times change; so at this point, insert The Name Of Your Choice, whoever's currently making headlines for some action* not *directlyconnected to his/her claim to fame: like Zsa Zsa's run-in with that cop, or Warren Beatty's latest romantic fling, or whatever;* do not *cite the details of the peccadillo, please; just the* name, *and let your* audience *figure the rest; otherwise you'll slow the show's pace to a dead stop!*]

DEX. You *read* that kind of trash?

CHARLENE. Only second-hand—it's Giddy's subscription. I don't get to look at it till she's drooled over it cover-to-cover! Hey, Dex, are you saying *you* don't read that kind of trash?

DEX. Why, no, of *course* I read it. It's just kinda fun to know *you* do, *too*! I mean, we're engaged—it forms a sort of *bond*!

CHARLENE. (*Interpreting correctly:*) The couple that *snoops* together *whoops* together?

DEX. (*Starts cuddling cozily with her*) Something like that.

BRET. (*Now garbed in that red velvet pants-suit*) All set! How do I look?

CHARLENE. (*Glances over her shoulder at him*) Like a raspberry popsicle!

GIDDY. (*Arm-in-arm with BRET now, leading him toward still-open front door*) You know, that's what *Father* always said about it!

BRET. No *wonder* your mother couldn't stand it! (*They exit, shutting door behind them.*)

JUD. (*Enters from kitchen, a potato chip in one hand, and glass of champagne in the other, strolls leisurely toward window*) Can't find the can-opener for the oysters, and this champagne is flat.

CHARLENE. (*Gets up from sofa, starts kitchenward*) Any *other* little compliments for the chef?

JUD. You're *not* the chef. *I* just put our dinner in the oven!

DEX. And left it to fend for itself?

JUD. (*Solemnly.*) A Watched Microwave Never Dings. (*Continues toward window*)

DEX. (*Glances toward armchair, stands*) Hey, I think I found your magazine! What page was that article on?

CHARLENE. I forget the page. But where's the magazine?

DEX. Right here! I'll get it—(*Takes hold of magazine-corner protruding from beneath armchair-cushion [see PRODUCTION NOTES], slips it out, starts paging through it*) Must be an *index* in here someplace ...

CHARLENE. (*Has ceased kitchenward move, returns to look over his shoulder as he pages, then reacts to something she sees in magazine, on:*) Oh! Oh no! (*Grabs magazine from him, and as he now looks over her shoulder at it:*) Does that gentleman's face look familiar?!

DEX. It's *Bret*! Bret *Fleming*!

CHARLENE. (*Almost a groan of chagrin*) And look what it says *under* his picture—!

DEX. (*Reads aloud, in some bafflement*) "America's Richest and Most Eligible Bachelor to Attend Boston Marathon"! (*Frowns, puzzled, turns to CHARLENE*) I thought you said Giddy always read this *cover-to-cover, before* you got to look at it? If you're partway *through* it already—she must have *read* it. But—how could she have *missed* this item?

CHARLENE. (*Gives him pitying look*) Dex ... honey ... what makes you think she *did* miss reading it?

DEX. (*Laughs as if she were kidding*) Come *on*, Charlene! Why, *that* would mean— (*His merriment fades a bit*) —that from the moment she saw him in the street— (*His merriment is now stunned realization*) —that she *knew*—knew all *along*—that Bret was—was—?

CHARLENE. (*With grim admiration of GIDDY's ploy*) The marital catch of the millenium! (*Tosses magazine aside in disgust*) Why didn't I see what she was up to? Why?!

DEX. (*Soothingly, placing arm across her shoulder*) Because *you're* a *normal* woman—no wiles, no deceits, no tricks, no ploys, no mental problems—

JUD. (*Who has paused en route toward window, just D of foyer, listening*) You call that a *normal* woman?!

DEX. (*Defensively*) Of course I do! I mean, heck, *my* picture was in this *very* magazine, just about *one* year ago, and—and— (*As he pauses, frowning with sudden suspicion, CHARLENE's face becomes a study in trapped terror for one instant; then, as DEX turns to her:*)

CHARLENE. (*Instantly brisk, cheery and nonchalant, starts for kitchen*) Wellllll, time to check the microwave!

DEX. Charlene Lockwood—

CHARLENE. (*Turns to face him, her voice low and peeping with dread*) Yes ... honey ... sweetie ... darling ...?

JUD. Should I leave the room?

DEX. You'd *miss* the chance to eyewitness a *murder?* What kind of cop *are* you?

CHARLENE. Aw, Dex...!

DEX. (*Moving toward her*) Charlene—!

CHARLENE. But honey, you *needed* CPR that day—!

DEX. (*Now face-to-face with her*) Yeah, sure. And then, when your mouth-to-mouth resuscitation got out of hand—

CHARLENE. *That* part was *your* fault! You revived faster than I expected, and—

DEX. (*Grips her upper arms*) You know—I never *did* find out who *pushed* me into the swimming pool...!

CHARLENE. (*Uneasily*) But—do you *care* ... do you *really* care—?

DEX. (*With a different, much more romantic meaning:*) Yes. I really care. I care a lot. (*His arms go around her*) An *awful* lot! You sly, underhanded, conniving, scheming—

CHARLENE. You forgot "beautiful" ...

DEX. (*Laughs*) You clown! (*Then, just as both are zeroing in for a terrific kiss:*)

JUD. (*Glances out window, reacts, looks out more intently*) That's the darnedest thing?!

CHARLENE. *What* is?

JUD. In the window of that townhouse across the street—

DEX. Something unusual?

JUD. (*Turns to face them*) *I've* never seen anything like it!

CHARLENE. What's *in* the window?

JUD. *Twelve* little old ladies with binoculars ... And they're all looking over here! What goes *on* in this apartment, *anyhow*, to draw a crowd like *that?!*

CHARLENE. (*Serene in DEX's embrace*) You'd be surprised, Officer Keegan, you'd be surprised!

(*And then as CHARLENE and DEX complete that clinch, and a wildly curious JUD turns to once again peer out the window in puzzlement—*)

THE CURTAIN FALLS

End of Play

PRODUCTION NOTES

BRET'S UNDERSHORTS: These should be neither boxer-style nor Jockey-style, one being too long, the other being too short, to "pass" for runner's shorts. There is a style of colorful undershorts that's almost undetectable from basketball-style shorts. This is the kind you should be using for his costuming. His tanktop should be colored, too, not simple white. Remember, we want him to *look* (except for those dress shoes) as if he *could* be a race-entrant in the marathon.

WINDOW CURTAINS: Since these must always *drop back* into place after peek-outs in Act I, but remain *open* after GIDDY shoves them aside in Act II, you should have them *pinned* together at curtain-rod level in the first act, and then *remove* the pin during the intermission so that they'll slide apart *permanently* in the second act and stay that way.

THE MAGAZINE: When GIDDY tosses it under the armchair-cushion in Act I, she needn't strive to keep a corner jutting out in view; matter of fact, since we want the audience to *forget* this magazine till the crucial final moments of the play, she should make sure it's well *back* on the seat under the cushion before she covers it. Then, at intermission, have it moved forward with just a corner visible (not *too* visible; just enough so DEX can see where it's at) near the upstage end of the cushion, so DEX doesn't have to delay the play's action by trying to *find* it when its time comes to re-appear. (If it *does* show, don't worry about it; any audience-members who might spot its corner jutting out in Act II will certainly not attach any *importance* to it.) The *identity* of your magazine can go one of two ways: You can either use a pleasantly flashy-and-gossipy magazine like *PEOPLE*—or (for obvious reasons) go the more *direct* route and use a magazine like *MONEY*. In the latter case, however, make sure the audience does *not* see the magazine's *name* when GIDDY stashes it; no point in telegraphing the show's comic *punch,* after all!

THE UPSTAGE DOOR: Pay *particular* attention to the stage-directions as to when this door is closed by a player or *not* closed by a player, so that certain moments in the play (such as JUD's appearance at the end of Act I) won't have to be hampered by frantic ad-libbing to account for someone *opening* the door for these moments. Let those stage-directions be your guide.

IF YOU ABSOLUTELY *MUST* HAVE THREE ACTS: Since in a comedy an act must end with a climatic laugh at a logical "resting place" for the audience, here is the way (and no other way will be approved) to break the show into three acts instead of two: First off, eliminate the existing curtain—but be *sure* GIDDY/BRET hold that kiss for a *minimum* of five seconds, so subsequent comments will make sense. Okay, *now* alter your *program* to read thusly:

> ACT I: very late in the afternoon
> ACT II: two seconds *earlier*
> ACT III: *four* seconds earlier

In other words, we are going to *backstep* a line or so to kick off Acts II and III, so the pace/thrust/timing established won't be lost and have to be re-achieved. Now, here is *exactly* the way this must be handled: Right after GIDDY shouts "*Antonio!*" and BRET reacts "I'm Italian?!" and she carols "Oh, I *knew* it! I just *knew* it!" and embraces him—*hold* the embrace and bring your curtain down to end Act I. Then, when you begin Act II, backtrack slightly, and have curtain rise with GIDDY's post-"*Antonio!*" embrace of BRET already established *en tableau* (her arms about him, her right cheek against his chest, her eyes closed, her smile rapturous), and the first line of Act II will be BRET's out-to-the-audience gasp of "I'm *Italian*?!", and then pick up exactly where you were and continue through I-just-knew-it/Carissima!/etc. Now continue on *through* what *had* been the first-act curtain (going from BRET's "Maybe I've been hasty" right into the BRET/GIDDY kiss [and *hold* for five seconds], then on to CHARLENE's "Hit me again." etc. through her "Try and stop me" line, at which time that five-second clinch breaks). Got all this? Okay, now for your *next* curtain: Halfway through BRET's surreptitious first conversation on the phone with Jacobsen, go as far as his wistful, hopeful, plaintive delivery of "Do *I* look *Italian*?!..." and have him *hold* that pose, and drop your curtain, ending Act II. When you raise the curtain on Act III, BRET will be on phone in *exact* attitude indicated in the stage-directions *preceding* that new Act II curtain-line, and do *all* the business indicated therein (*very* surreptitious look bedroomward [etc.]), *taking his time* about it, and *then* he will deliver his "Do *I* look *Italian*?!..." line, do *all* the indicated business in the *next* stage-direction through his "*Grazie!*", and this will re-establish the plot-energy fully for the audience, and then you can proceed with the act as written through the final curtain of the show. Under *no* circumstances will you break this show into three acts at any *other* spots or in any other *manner*, got that? Fine. Happy playing.

CAST-AGES: There is *no* reason CHARLENE and DEX cannot be a *middle-aged* couple, if you prefer.

- Stage Setting -
"I TAKE THIS MAN"